"As Scarlett O'Hara said, 'Tomorrow's another day.'"

Resolved, Kristin reached around him to grab her purse. Zach caught her hand.

Kristin stopped breathing as he moved closer, his gray eyes telegraphing his intent and giving her ample time to refuse the kiss she knew was coming. Her heart banged against her rib cage as he slid his hands inside her open jacket and coaxed her to him.

Why wasn't she pushing him away? Why wasn't she telling him that he had no right to touch her anymore?

She had no answers. Because she was suddenly too involved in the texture and feel of him to care. It had been so long since she'd felt like this. She'd been sure that a normal physical response was dead to her forever. And yet, here it was…that nervous quiver, that breathless tremble, that downward whoosh of the Ferris wheel.

Then instinct took over, memories took over, and they came together in a hard, hungry kiss that was an explosion of heat and hormones

Dear Reader,

July is a sizzling month both outside *and* in, and once again we've rounded up six exciting titles to keep your temperature rising. It all starts with the latest addition to Marilyn Pappano's HEARTBREAK CANYON miniseries, *Lawman's Redemption*, in which a brooding man needs help connecting with the lonely young girl who just might be his daughter—and he finds it in the form of a woman with similar scars in her romantic past. Don't miss this emotional, suspenseful read.

Eileen Wilks provides the next installment in our twelve-book miniseries, ROMANCING THE CROWN, with *Her Lord Protector*. Fireworks ensue when a Montebellan lord has to investigate a beautiful commoner who may be a friend—or a foe!—of the royal family. This miniseries just gets more and more intriguing. And Kathleen Creighton finishes up her latest installment of her INTO THE HEARTLAND miniseries with *The Black Sheep's Baby*. A freewheeling photojournalist who left town years ago returns—with a little pink bundle strapped to his chest, and a beautiful attorney in hot pursuit. In Marilyn Tracy's *Cowboy Under Cover*, a grief-stricken widow who has set up a haven for children in need of rescue finds herself with that same need—and her rescuer is a handsome federal marshal posing as a cowboy. Nina Bruhns is back with *Sweet Revenge*, the story of a straitlaced woman posing as her wild identical twin—and now missing—sister to learn of her fate, who in the process hooks up with the seductive detective who is also searching for her. And in *Bachelor in Blue Jeans* by Lauren Nichols, during a bachelor auction, a woman inexplicably bids on the man who once spurned her, and wins—or does she? This reunion romance will break your heart.

So get a cold drink, sit down, put your feet up and enjoy them all—and don't forget to come back next month for more of the most exciting romance reading around…only in Silhouette Intimate Moments.

Yours,

Leslie J. Wainger
Executive Senior Editor

Please address questions and book requests to:
Silhouette Reader Service
U.S.: 3010 Walden Ave., P.O. Box 1325, Buffalo, NY 14269
Canadian: P.O. Box 609, Fort Erie, Ont. L2A 5X3

Bachelor in Blue Jeans
LAUREN NICHOLS

INTIMATE MOMENTS™

Published by Silhouette Books

America's Publisher of Contemporary Romance

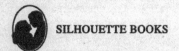

SILHOUETTE BOOKS

ISBN 0-373-27234-0

BACHELOR IN BLUE JEANS

Books by Lauren Nichols

Silhouette Intimate Moments

Accidental Heiress #840
Accidental Hero #893
Accidental Father #994
Bachelor in Blue Jeans #1164

LAUREN NICHOLS

Lauren Nichols started writing by accident, so it seems fitting that the word *accidental* appears in her first three titles for Silhouette. Once eager to illustrate children's books, she tried to get her foot in that door, only to learn that most publishing houses use their own artists. Then one publisher offered to look at her sketches if she also wrote the tale. During the penning of that story, Lauren fell head over heels in love with writing fiction.

In addition to writing novels, Lauren's romance and mystery short stories have appeared in several leading magazines. She counts her family and friends as her greatest treasures, and strongly believes in the Beatles' philosophy, "All You Need Is Love." When this Pennsylvania author isn't writing or trying unsuccessfully to give up French vanilla cappuccino, she's traveling or hanging out with her very best friend—her husband, Mike.

This book is for my brother Bill and my aunt Buckey,
who have left this world for a better one.
I love and miss you both.

And for my good friend and always-smiling
cappuccino buddy, Jeanne Hassleman.

And last but not least, for Taylor Nicole Haight,
the newest addition to our family.
Welcome to the world, little sweetheart.

Chapter 1

Zach Davis scowled, his humiliation building as shrieking women beyond the velvet curtain nearly drowned out the bump-and-grind music blasting from a speaker somewhere.

God help him.

God help every bachelor on the auction block this evening.

Releasing an exasperated breath, he glared down at his tiny great-aunt as she continued to fuss with the boutonniere on his tux. The tux some other poor sap should've been wearing.

"Aunt Etta, I swear, if I'd known why you wanted me to come over here tonight, I would've packed my truck and headed straight back to Nags Head."

Etta Gardner sent him a delighted smile, her sweet, musical voice fueling his irritation. "Nonsense, dear. You'd never leave my porches in the sorry state they're in. Why, however would I sell my house?"

She reached high to pat his cheek. "I know you're distressed about this, but who was I to call? The bachelor who cancelled was very tall and quite brawny. You were the only person I could think of who could wear his tuxedo."

Zach yanked down his shirt cuffs. "Lucky me."

"Gracious, no! Lucky *us* that you were back in town!" Etta winced then, and quickly lowered her voice—presumably so she wasn't overheard in the lavish country club's crowded dining room.

She needn't have worried. Though the foyer-turned-staging area where they stood was adjacent to the dining room, it was like Mardi Gras in there—loud and frenzied. Zach doubted the women could even hear each other.

"Just remember that tonight's proceeds will give our needy children a lovely Christmas this year," Etta continued, "and you'll do just fine."

The tag "needy children" hit home, conjuring thoughts Zach didn't like to think about. He willed them away as Etta took a step back to assess him through her rimless bifocals.

Zach regarded her at the same time, his heart warming despite the untenable spot she'd put him in. The skinny little woman who'd shown him what love was and saved him from foster care wore a filmy-looking pink and blue flowered dress and sensible white shoes. The blue tips on her carnation corsage nearly matched the tint in her cap-cut hair.

"Very *nice,* dear," she gushed. "Of course, it's too bad you didn't have time for a shave and a trim before you came over, but I've heard that some young women go for that lumberjack look. Now, how does the tux feel?"

"Frustrated and manipulated, just like the guy wearing it."

Zach hooked an index finger inside his collar, gritting his teeth when his fingernail scraped his Adam's apple. "And why does this collar have to be so tight? I probably have ligature marks on my neck."

Etta shooed his hands away. "It's not tight, it's perfect. Don't you dare spoil the lovely line of your bow tie." In a flash, her smile returned, mischief brimming in her blue eyes. "Mark my words. You'll thank me for this one day."

"Right," he grumbled. "What man wouldn't want to look like an idiot in front of a bunch of people he hasn't seen in thirteen years?"

Just then, the rowdy female auctioneer behind the curtain bellowed out a number, and Etta's interest in turning him into something he wasn't, fled. Scurrying to the ramp leading to the curtained-off runway, she beckoned to the bachelor who was next in line. Chad Hollister bent to hear Etta's instructions.

Zach sent Hollister another cold once-over. He and Hollister had exchanged greetings when Zach arrived a few minutes ago, but they both knew it was all for show. They'd never liked each other. Not in high school, and not now. Blond, polished Chad had been the antithesis of everything Zach had been and still was—Joe College to Zach's school of hard knocks. The town's golden boy to Zach's working stiff. Girls had flocked to Hollister like gulls to French fries. He'd had it all...expensive clothes, a flashy car and moneyed parents.

He and Zach wouldn't have had a reason in the world to say hello to each other, much less cross

swords, except they'd both fallen hard for the same
girl.

Kristin.

Zach glanced back at Etta, who was wrapping up
her speech in a loud stage whisper. "As soon as you're
sold, go directly to the woman who bought you, and
sit at her table. And be charming, Chad. We want these
ladies to bid high."

Hollister sent her a sly wink and a sexy drawl.
"Don't worry, Mrs. Gardner. I'll get every dime they
have left in their pocketbooks." Then the auctioneer
called Hollister's name, and Wisdom, Pennsylvania's
handsome young police chief burst through the red
velvet curtain with a killer attitude and a cocky grin.

The shrieking in the dining room reached new
heights.

Zach turned away in disgust, digging inside his collar again. What was it people said? The more things
changed, the more they remained the same? Being
fresh meat at this charity freak show didn't seem to
bother Hollister at all. But then, the jerk had always
loved the limelight.

Unbidden, an image flashed of Kristin and Chad
being crowned king and queen of their junior prom,
but Zach shoved it away, just as he'd beaten back that
disturbing reminder of his childhood. There was no
reason to dwell on those thoughts anymore. He was a
success now. He'd never have to feel ashamed again.

An explosion of applause and unladylike whistles
signaled that Hollister had been sold, and suddenly
Etta was nudging him up the ramp. "Your turn, dear.
Now, will you kindly *smile* when you get out there?"

No, he wouldn't. He'd be too busy praying for a
power failure that would empty the damn building.

"Zachary?"

"Yeah, yeah, I'm going," he muttered. Then, with a last impatient look at his aunt, he stepped through the curtain and onto an elevated runway lined with twinkle lights—and the room went wild.

He nearly bolted when the buxom auctioneer with the flame-red hair screeched over the melee, "My heavens, ladies, get out your checkbooks! Look what we have here! *Welcome home, Zach Davis!"*

Kristin's heart stopped and she jerked her gaze up from her coffee cup to stare at the man coming down the runway. For an instant, she couldn't breathe, couldn't think. It couldn't be.

But it was.

Maybelle Parker's boisterous voice grated over the continued applause and randy music. "We've got prime cut, grade-A stuff here! Zach's a thirty-three-year-old contractor with his own business in North Carolina's Outer Banks. And aren't we lucky that he's here visiting his aunt for a few weeks! We can gawk at him even *after* the auction!"

Someone started dinging a glass with a spoon, and half the room followed suit.

"I don't have to tell you he's gorgeous," Maybelle yelled into the mike. "You can see that for yourselves. Now let's show our hometown boy how much we appreciate his help with our local charity!"

"Twenty-five dollars!" someone shrieked from across the room.

"Thirty!" Grace Thornberry shouted from Kristin's own table.

Feeling faintly sick, Kristin tried to block out the bidding in five-dollar increments that would keep him on the runway forever. But she couldn't block him out. Zach seemed to come forward in slow motion.

This was no boy, she thought, despite Maybelle's description. He was nothing like the gangly nineteen-year-old she'd loved. His teenage good looks had ripened and matured into broad shoulders, a rugged, angular face and a sexy shag of coal-black hair.

One thing hadn't changed, though, she realized, seeing the trapped look beneath his brooding expression. He'd never liked being the center of attention—preferred to stay in the shadows where people couldn't look too closely and make comparisons between him and his father.

So why was he parading himself this way? What could possibly make him want to stand up there in front of a hundred women who'd left responsibility and good taste at the door?

The shouts kept coming. "Zach! Open your jacket!"

"Turn around!"

"Shake your booty!"

He stood stone still.

Suddenly a rush of compassion washed through Kristin and she felt every ounce of his humiliation. He'd hurt her more terribly than she could ever describe. He'd betrayed her and he'd lied to her, and it had been months before she'd been able to breathe again without pain.

Yet in spite of that, she was recalling a time when he'd held her in the loft of his aunt Etta's barn and murmured that she was everything to him. Every dream he'd ever had...every wish he'd ever made.

"I—three hundred dollars!"

A hush settled over the room, and every lined, shadowed and mascaraed eye turned to Kristin. Panic nearly immobilized her. *Had she said that? How could she have said that?*

Maybelle gaped in shock. "Did you say three hundred dollars, Kristin?"

Kristin nodded numbly, utterly mortified by her outburst. "Yes, I... Is that enough?" *Dear God, how was she going to get out of this with even a shred of dignity?*

Maybelle's rowdy laughter ricocheted off the walls, and to Kristin's chagrin, was joined by everyone else's. "Well, I don't know! I *think* so! Ladies, I have three hundred once! Twice! Come on, if he's worth three, he's *got* to be worth four!" Then, "Sold to Ms. Kristin Chase for three hundred dollars!"

"Three hundred dollars, Kristin?" Grace Thornberry called laughingly from across the table. "My goodness, it's been a long time for you, hasn't it?"

With a red-faced smile for her teasing tablemates, Kristin grabbed her black beaded bag and walked quickly to the podium to give Maybelle a check. She was ruined. Anyone who knew her past with Zach would label her a doormat. Especially Chad.

She slanted a veiled glance at him as she handed the check to Maybelle. Chad was angry and he wasn't trying to hide it—not a very chivalrous thing to do with Mary Alice Hampton draped all over him. Kristin regretted his disappointment, but she hadn't bid on him for a purpose. She wanted him to find someone to love—someone wonderful who could love him back.

"Thank you, dear!" Maybelle gushed effusively. "Now scoot on back to your table and grab that handsome man!"

Kristin blanched at the thought. No way. She had no idea what she was going to say to him, and she wouldn't have her embarrassment and fumbling witnessed by Grace and the others.

Scraping together what remained of her poise, Kristin strode to the back of the room. She hadn't wanted to come here tonight, had always considered these kinds of things tacky and dehumanizing. But as the director of Wisdom's Small Business Association, one of the auction's sponsors, she was almost obligated to attend.

Now she wished she'd insisted that someone else take her place this evening.

Fighting the urge to finger-comb her short auburn hair, she watched Zach walk toward her, stop to accept Maybelle's over-the-top thanks, then continue forward with slow, deliberate strides.

It disturbed her to realize that seeing him again could electrify her nerve endings, harden her heart and shatter it, all at the same time.

He stopped several feet from her. "Hello, Kristin," he said politely.

She managed to keep her voice from trembling. "Hello, Zach. You're looking well."

"You, too."

"Thank you." Apparently, they were going to be civil.

He'd only been back a few times since her mother's death nine years ago, generally during the holidays to visit his aunt Etta. But this was the first time she'd seen him since the funeral. She was unprepared for the changes that years of working outdoors had created. Though it was barely June, his rugged face was deeply tanned, with faint lines bracketing his mouth and creasing the skin beside his gray eyes. And though he'd always been tall, he now had a powerfully built body that not even the classic lines of a tuxedo could hide.

Like warning buoys, those old feelings of hurt and resentment tipped and bobbed in the wide gulf between them. And impossibly, beneath those emotions, the undertow of attraction still pulled. Kristin read the look in his eyes and knew he felt it, too. But he didn't welcome it.

"Why me?" he asked after the silence had stretched out as long as either of them could tolerate it. "God knows there were enough other men you could've bid on. Even good old Chad." His mouth thinned. "Or was there something you neglected to say the last time we spoke?"

No, she'd said every harsh, hurtful thing that was in her heart the day of her mother's funeral. It had been wrong, but seeing him at the cemetery after two devastating weeks at the hospital watching her mother slowly slip away was more than she could take. His presence had only made her feel worse.

"Actually, I'd planned to bid on someone else," she lied, unwilling to let him know he still got to her. "Unfortunately, I was in the ladies' room when he was auctioned off. You were my last chance to donate to the Children's Christmas Fund."

He eyed her skeptically. "The people running this shindig wouldn't accept a straight donation? No charity I know operates that way."

Kristin released a sigh. She'd never been good at lying. That was his talent. "All right. I felt sorry for you, too."

A nerve leapt in his jaw. "You felt *sorry* for me?"

"Yes." She knew how he felt about pity, but the

truth wouldn't have been necessary if he'd been gentleman enough to accept her first answer. "I saw how uncomfortable you were, and for a second, I remembered that we were friends once. I wanted you off the runway."

"That's it?"

"That's it." She wouldn't let him think all was forgiven when nothing was further from the truth. "It was just a knee-jerk reaction. If I had it to do over again, I probably wouldn't have."

His gray gaze went flat. "I'll send you a check in the morning to cover your bid."

"There's no need to do that."

"Yes, there is. If you remember anything about me, you know I don't like owing people. I had enough of that when I was putting off bill collectors for my old man."

"This isn't a debt, Zach."

"It feels like one. After all, you did get me off the runway—and you didn't get the man you wanted. I'll mail the check to your shop."

"I'll send it right back," she said, and started away.

Zach grabbed her hand. He released it quickly when a shock jolted them both.

Kristin's heart raced as they stared at each other. *It's just static,* she told herself. *Just static electricity from the carpet.*

The moment stretched out on tenterhooks. Then Zach's voice softened, reminding her that they hadn't always been distant with each other. "It never changes between us, does it, Kris? Even after all these years, sparks still fly the second we—"

She couldn't listen to this. "I have to go. Goodbye, Zach."

Then she strode back toward the table groupings, her stomach quaking, and every nerve ending in her body wound like a steel spring. It was illogical, irrational and unbelievable, but as much as she despised what he'd done, the chemistry they'd surrendered to the summer of their senior year was still strong, still fierce, still dangerously tempting.

And she resented it.

Zach watched her wave and smile to friends as she hurried toward the opposite end of the room, then stopped to talk to three women who'd risen to corral her. He was finally free to take a good long look. His gaze slid appreciatively over her narrow back, over the flare of her hips in the sleeveless black dress she wore, then slipped down her long, shapely legs. He took in her hair again. It was short now—not much longer than his—but silky bangs still fell below her brows, framing her wide, beautiful brown eyes. They were the confident eyes of a woman now, he decided. Clear, intelligent…and unforgiving.

He jammed his hands into his trouser pockets. He'd thought his mood couldn't get any blacker when Etta met him at the door with the damn tux. He'd been wrong.

"Well," Etta said wistfully, magically appearing as though he'd conjured her up. "That certainly didn't go as well as I'd planned."

With difficulty, Zach pulled his gaze from Kristin and glanced down at his great-aunt's rueful expression. "What didn't go well? The auction?"

She slipped an arm through his. "No, dear, your meeting with Kristin. I'd hoped it would be a little friendlier, but I suppose with all that's between you, it was too much to hope for. Maybe you should stop by her shop tomorrow and try again.''

Everything in Zach stilled as he stared down at his elfin aunt, and his mind took him on a slow, sure path to trickery and deceit. ''Aunt Etta, what did you do?''

''Come dear,'' she said, patting his arm. ''Let's have some dessert.''

Zach stood his ground. ''I don't want dessert, I want an explanation. What did you do?''

But she was already walking toward a table where blueberry cheesecake and coffee sat untouched in front of six empty chairs. Swearing beneath his breath, Zach followed, seated her, then took the chair next to her. ''You set me up! There *was* no sick bachelor. That's why you wanted me here a day early.''

Without a trace of apology, Etta placed a white linen napkin on her lap. ''Honestly, Zachary, we should all be grateful you decided to go into the construction business. You'd have made a dreadful detective. Didn't you wonder why your tuxedo fit so well? The jacket, the trousers—*the size fourteen shoes?*''

No, he hadn't, but then, he'd never expected Etta to bamboozle him, either. ''Could we forget my deductive powers for the moment? Why in *hell* would you feel the need to drag me down here and put me through this?''

''Because I've waited years for you to marry a nice girl and bring some children into this world before I'm gone, and I'm running out of patience. When you offered to come home and get the farmhouse ready to sell, I decided that a bit of meddling was justified if it got you and Kristin talking again. It's time.''

Zach narrowed his eyes, trying his best to follow Etta's reasoning. *''You expect me to marry Kris?''*

He'd have to be certifiable to want a woman who'd put his heart through a Cuisinart not once, but twice.

"Good heavens, no! She's still mad, and I don't blame her." Etta shook her fork at him. "You need closure, young man. That's what they say on the talk shows. Kristin does, too, if that three-hundred-dollar bid is any indication. The two of you need to resolve this unfinished business between you so you can get on with your lives."

"Aunt Etta, I don't need closure, I need ten more hours in the day. And I'm sorry to disappoint you, but I don't have the time or the inclination to marry and start a family right now. I've got a construction business to run. As a matter of fact," he added, glancing toward the exit, "I—"

He stopped abruptly as a couple separated from the small crowd that had gathered at the front of the room. Then, as he watched, Chad Hollister escorted Kristin though the wide archway and out of sight.

The words she'd said not ten minutes ago came back to him. This time he gave them more credence. *Actually, I'd planned to bid on someone else, but I was in the ladies' room when he was auctioned off.*

Chad Hollister was "someone else?" *Chad Hollister?*

"As a matter of fact, you what?" Etta prompted.

Zach sent her a grim look and pushed to his feet. "As a matter of fact, I do have unfinished business. I was tearing off the front porch when you phoned with this trumped up emergency of yours. I need to get back to it."

"Zachary, it's dark, and the power and water won't be turned on until Monday. What are you planning to use for light? Fireflies?"

He smiled. "No, Aunt Smarty-pants, I brought a generator with me. You're catching a ride back to the high-rise with your friends, right?"

"Yes, and I wish you'd reconsider staying there with me. At least until the utilities are reconnected."

"Again, thank you for the offer, but I'm fine where I am. With my work habits, you don't need me stomping through your apartment in the middle of the night disrupting your sleep."

He bent to kiss her cheek. "I'll see you tomorrow evening for dinner. We'll drive into Lancaster—maybe go to that Amish farmhouse restaurant with the great chicken."

"Go see Kristin," Etta said ignoring his invitation. "She bought the souvenir shop on Main Street where she worked in high school and turned it into a lovely place—Forget Me Not Antiques."

"Aunt Etta—"

"It's not often a person gets a chance to right the wrongs from their past."

Zach met her eyes candidly. "If I had any wrongs to right, I'd do it. I don't. See you tomorrow for dinner."

Ten minutes later, he'd left the tux behind and was striding across the parking lot beneath a starry summer sky, and feeling damn good to be in jeans again.

He wasn't a tux man. He was a sweat and calluses, hammer and nails man. Now, Hollister—he was a tux man. Hollister with his fake smile, military bearing and swaggering attitude. Good God, what did Kris see in that jerk? Position? Education? It sure as hell couldn't be personality. Hollister had been mean-spirited and cocky from the day they'd met in the same tenth grade homeroom—a kid with money who'd enjoyed lording it over the kids without. Not that Zach gave a fat fig who she dated. He'd just always thought she'd be more selective when she hooked up with someone else.

Climbing inside his truck and firing the engine, he drove toward Etta's old farmhouse on the outskirts of town.

Though he tried to ignore it, his past swung hard at him from every bend in the road. He approached the tiny stone church Kristin had coaxed him into attending, back when he'd decided to change his bad boy image and do whatever it took to keep her. He'd taken some serious heat from his friends for that, but he hadn't cared. The sign out front evoked a near-smile. Come In. We're Prayer Conditioned.

Traffic got heavier when he reached the brightly lit shopping plaza that hadn't been there in his youth, then tapered off again when he turned down a secondary road toward the "poor end" of town. He passed four houses that needed work, then slowed the truck when he got to the empty lot where the hovel he'd once lived in had stood.

There'd been no flowers on the table in that place, no clean sheets on the beds, no mother with hot meals after school. She'd cut and run when he was seven and they were living somewhere in New Mexico. A long string of different states and different flophouses had come after that, and somewhere along the line, he'd missed two whole years of school.

By the time they'd finally made their way back here—back *home,* his father had called it, though no brass band had shown up to meet them—Zach was fifteen and understood clearly why his mother took off.

But by then, he'd built up a dandy kiss-my-ass attitude. He'd been way too cool to let anyone know how it shamed him to be Hap Davis's son, and fifteen— not thirteen—in the eighth grade.

He saw his father again, sitting in the recliner in their pan-gray living room, empty beer bottles lined up on the floor beside him. He was glad someone had torn down the old shack. Otherwise, he might've been tempted to buy it and rip it down himself.

Zach clicked on a country music station and rolled down the window to let in the night air.

His usual expectations upon returning home had been met. He'd only been back a few hours, and he was already primed to leave.

Chapter 2

Kristin stepped out of the shower, wrapped herself in a white terry robe, then with a vengeance, rubbed a towel over her short hair. She was so churned up, she didn't know what to do with herself. Flinging the towel over the shower curtain rod, she strode barefoot into her pretty oak kitchen where her teakettle was screaming its spout off. She turned off the gas.

How could she have let him get to her like that?

What had *possessed* her to bid three hundred dollars on a man who'd crushed her spirit, and for months, had her gobbling chocolate like a child on Halloween?

She fixed her tea, grabbed the cookie jar from the countertop and carried it to the sofa in her living room. After a moment, she picked up the phone to call Rachel in Flagstaff. She hung up before she'd finished dialing the area code.

The second she told Rachel that she'd seen Zach again, her psychologist-sister would either counsel

Kristin to death over the phone or catch the next plane home and do it in person.

Kristin couldn't handle any more preaching tonight. Not after Chad's well-meaning diatribe when he walked her to her car. He'd pretended concern, but his underlying feelings were easy to read. He was hurt, and he couldn't understand how she could have bid on a man she supposedly despised. He hadn't been in the best of moods when she'd sent him back to Mary Alice.

Kristin reached inside the cookie jar and grabbed a handful of Oreos. She needed to forget that Zach Davis ever existed. She needed to drink tea and eat cookies and watch mindless TV and forget.

It was simply mind over matter. She'd done it before, and she could do it again.

The next morning as she said goodbye to Mildred Arnett and hung up the phone in her shop, Kristin was teeming with energy. This mind over matter thing was easy. All she'd needed to do was focus directly on the work she loved, and she'd been doing that nonstop for an hour—ever since she came in at seven-thirty.

Pushing to her feet, Kristin grabbed the shipping manifest from her clipboard and strode into the small stockroom off her sales floor to finish checking in the previous day's delivery. Two dozen cartons were stacked beside the metal door leading to the alley.

Pulling a stool close, she opened the boxes, checking each one to see that the description and number of items agreed with the manifest, then noting it on the sheet and boxing the items back up to be shelved later.

The very last carton was a case of jelly-jar candles

she'd received from a new vendor. Kristin took more time with them, removing the lids to check the quality and strength of the fragrances. The second she opened the strawberry candle with the pretty red-speckled label, she knew it was a mistake.

One whiff had tears filling her eyes and that cruel videotape in her mind clicking on again.

Suddenly she was driving up the bumpy dirt driveway to Etta Gardner's farmhouse again…guiding her mother's car to the end, then back behind the big, white clapboard house where the strawberry fields opened and a small campfire blazed orange in the darkness.

The scent of strawberries filled her mind and lungs, and Kristin's chest began to ache. Because there was Zach in the car's headlights again, shattering her heart in a million pieces.

The bell over the entry door jerked Kristin out of her thoughts, and blinking rapidly, she blessed the interruption. She didn't need this anymore, didn't want it.

Smoothing her pearl-gray jacket over her white camisole and gray skirt, she summoned a smile and returned to her sales floor where antiques and pretty collectibles shared space with Amish baked goods, silk flowers and more candles.

Her face froze when she saw who'd entered. Then she reminded herself that she was a professional, drew a steadying breath and walked out to greet Zach, just as she would greet any other customer who walked through her door.

"Good morning, Kris."

"Good morning." She would not get upset again. She would not run trembling to the cookie jar ever again because of him. She stepped behind the glass showcase that served as a sales counter to stand beside the hulking old-fashioned silver cash register. "What can I do for you?"

"Nothing. I'm here to do something for you." He was dressed in snug, faded jeans and a white knit polo shirt with an open collar that showcased his broad shoulders and tanned arms. His steady gaze held hers as he reached for his wallet, withdrew a check, and laid it on the counter.

She knew without looking that it was made out to her in the amount of three hundred dollars. "I told you last night that I didn't want it."

"And I told you that I don't like owing people. Take it."

"No."

He shoved it under the cash register. "All right, then add it to your donation or use it for a bookmark."

She paused for a moment, then nodded, knowing that if she kept refusing, they'd be at this all day. "Thank you. I'll see that the hospital auxiliary gets it. Now, if there's nothing else, I need to get back to work."

"There is something else."

Kristin waited.

"Before we spoke last night, Maybelle Parker collared me."

"Yes, I know. I saw her."

"She said we were expected to join the other bachelors and their dates for a dinner cruise on Lake Edward in two weeks. Are you planning to go?"

She was stunned that he would even ask. "With you?"

"You did buy me."

Kristin kept her tone even. "I did not buy you, I made a donation to the Children's Christmas Fund. I thought you understood that."

"So you said. But it was a pretty hefty donation. Are you sure you didn't expect something more?"

This time she couldn't keep the edge out of her voice. "I have *no* expectations where you're concerned. I'm not going on the cruise. But if you're interested, by all means, feel free to ask someone else."

"I'm not interested." Zach returned his wallet to his back pocket. "I'll only be here for a few weeks, and I'll need most of that time to get my aunt's house in shape for a Realtor. I don't have time for cruises."

"Really?" she asked, irked again. "Would you have answered the same way if I'd said I *wanted* to attend?"

"Looking for a fight, Kris?" he asked curiously. "We used to be pretty good at it."

The arrival of another customer stopped her reply, and for the second time in minutes, Kristin was glad for the interruption. She was even happier to see Chad, but probably for all the wrong reasons.

"Hi," she called, smiling.

"Hi," Chad called back cheerfully. "You look pretty this morning. How's my best girl?"

"Full of energy," she answered, letting the "best girl" thing slide.

Zach watched Hollister amble toward them, happy to return the jerk's frigid nod as he carried a take-out bag to the sales counter. He eased as close to Kristin as the counter allowed, an intimate smile on his lips as he unloaded coffee in foam cups, stir sticks and creamers.

This morning, the chief was all decked out in his

uniform—dark gray shirt with black epaulets and pocket flaps, black pants, and lots of shiny silver buttons. There was more crime-fighting paraphernalia hanging from his utility belt than Batman's.

Zach found himself disliking Hollister more with every passing second. Maybe because he'd figuratively elbowed Zach out of the way. Or maybe because Chad was fixing Kristin's coffee from memory.

Hollister spoke cordially to Zach as he stirred cream into Kristin's cup, though there was no mistaking the "get lost" message in his green eyes. "Sorry, but I didn't bring enough for company. If I'd known you were here, I'd have ordered another cup."

Sure he would have. "Thanks just the same, but I've already had my quota for the day."

"Early riser, are you?"

The question sounded like an accusation. In fact, everything he said sounded like an accusation. Zach's edginess increased.

Kristin cleared her throat. "I had an interesting call from Anna Mae's cousin a few minutes ago, Chad. Apparently, all the legal issues have been wrapped up, and Mrs. Arnett's now free to sell the house and its contents."

Hollister handed her a foam cup. "Bet she's relieved to get on with it. She and her son have been back and forth a lot in the past few weeks." He frowned wryly. "Weird people, those two."

Zach stilled. How many Anna Maes could there be in a town this size? "Are you talking about Anna Mae Kimble?"

Chad took a cautious sip of hot coffee, then favored Zach with his attention again. "She was the department's secretary for years," he said sympathetically. "She passed away last month."

Zach felt a stab of regret as a childhood memory of Anna Mae moved through his mind, and once again he was grateful for her kindness. "What happened?"

"It was an accident," Chad said. "I don't like speaking ill of the dead, particularly when the deceased was a good friend. But apparently Anna Mae had a little too much sherry the night she died. She fell in her home. Struck her head on a coffee table."

The entry bell chimed again, and a solemn, bow-tied, older man Zach recognized entered the shop. Harlan Greene was the town's perennial tax collector, having served in that position for decades. According to Etta, he still held the job.

Harlan waved to them, then frowning, perused the selection of Amish baked goods.

Chad continued in a lower voice. "According to the coroner, Anna Mae died instantly."

"I'm sorry," Zach murmured, meaning it. "She was a nice woman." Nicer than a cocky teenage kid had deserved.

Harlan carried a package of cinnamon rolls to the counter and handed Kristin several bills. The sadness in his eyes was unmistakable. "She was the salt of the earth," he said. "Guess that Arnett woman will be sellin' off her things any day now."

"Looks that way," Chad replied, then glanced at Kristin. "I take it that's why Mrs. Arnett phoned you this morning?"

Kristin counted out Harlan's change, then nodded hesitantly, wishing Chad had waited until Harlan had gone to bring that up. "She wondered if I might be interested in buying a few of Anna Mae's pieces. I'm meeting her at the house this evening.''

"Won't find anything of value over there," Harlan said huskily, pocketing his coins. "Leastwise, nothing that would work in your shop." He picked up his rolls. "She liked frogs, was all. Frogs on her switch plates, frogs on the canister set, frogs all over the damn house." As he turned to leave, a bitter tone entered his voice. "No, you won't find anything worthwhile over there."

Kristin watched the door close behind him, then followed Harlan's path past her multipaned bay window until he disappeared. Touched, she turned to Chad. "Did you know about Anna Mae and Harlan?"

He nodded. "She liked him, but she didn't like his gambling. Gave him his walking papers shortly before she died." Chad glanced at the cuckoo clock on the wall. "Well, I'd better get to work. Dinner tonight?"

Kristin stared blankly at him. Where had that invitation come from? She also wondered at the offhanded way he'd asked—as if they dined together often, which wasn't the case.

She felt Zach's gaze on her, heavy and curious. Suddenly she was uneasy. "I'm sorry, but my plans with Mrs. Arnett aren't firm. I'll be touring the house at her convenience."

"Okay," Chad replied, shrugging. "I'll probably see you a little later anyhow. Maybe we can grab some ice cream or something."

"I...okay," she answered, still feeling off balance. "Thanks for the coffee."

"My pleasure. Always." But instead of leaving, Chad eased back against the counter to finish his coffee and sort through his keys. When he finally glanced up again, both his expression and tone had hardened.

"Why don't I walk you out, Davis? The sun's shining. Too beautiful a day to be stuck indoors if you don't have to be."

Zach's eyes were gray steel. "Why don't you walk yourself out, Hollister? I'm not ready to leave yet."

Startled, utterly bewildered, Kristin cast about for something to say, then hit the release lever on her cash register. The drawer dinged open, the tinny ring momentarily breaking their face-off. Whatever was going on here—idiotic male muscle flexing or a burst of rivalry from their past—it made her uncomfortable, and she wanted no part of it.

"You two do what you want," she said briskly and closed the cash drawer. "Stay or leave. I need to get some change from my safe and make a phone call."

Neither man commented, but Zach watched her go, shamelessly enjoying the view until she'd closed the door behind her. A sweet, wild wind stirred inside him.

"Pull your eyes back in their sockets, hotshot. You had your chance thirteen years ago, and you screwed it up."

Slowly, Zach turned to face Hollister again. "So you're the guy now?"

"That's right, I'm the guy."

"Fine with me," he replied, shrugging. "But I've noticed that she's not wearing a ring. I keep wondering what that means."

A nerve leapt in Hollister's jaw. "It *means* that Kristin and I have an understanding. For you, it means that you'd better observe all posted speed limits and put money in the parking meters. It also wouldn't be prudent to cross the street anywhere but at a cross-walk."

He glanced toward the door, then offered Zach a nasty smile. "You know, as I came inside, I noticed a black truck with Carolina tags parked out front. Think I'll run a check on the license plate—make sure the owner has no outstanding warrants. I might even glance at the inspection sticker."

"What's this?" Zach asked, trying not to laugh. "Police harassment?"

"Not at all. It's just a warning to an out-of-state visitor that when laws are broken in this town…I act."

This time Zach couldn't stop a smile. "And I'll bet you do a damn fine job of it."

Hollister's face turned crimson. "Just watch your step," he said coldly. "You don't want me for an enemy." Then he was stalking out of the shop, leaving Zach to wonder if Chad's blustering was a territory-marking thing…or insecurity because he *had* no hold on Kristin.

Not that he cared, either way.

Kristin said goodbye to Mildred Arnett, drew a tentative breath, then slowly opened the door to her office and looked around. The silence was an enormous relief.

Grateful that they'd gone, she added change to her cash drawer, retrieved her glass cleaner and paper towels from beneath a counter, then walked to her bay window. There, dolls in Victorian costumes sat at a mock tea party, flanked by a profusion of plumed hats, Bavarian china, flowers and silk. She stepped up into the display, squirted a few tiny glass panes, and started to wipe.

A low deep voice shattered her composure.

"What's this? A jewelry box?"

Kristin turned around slowly to see Zach standing beside a tall armoire with his back to her. An unwelcome warmth flowed through her as he reached for an antique music box on a high shelf, and she watched the subtle play of muscle and sinew beneath his shirt.

"It…it can be," she replied, swallowing. Setting her cleaner and paper towels aside, she stepped down from the display. He was a customer, she told herself again. She would show him what he wanted to see— then she would show him the door.

Zach raised the footed box's filigreed silver lid, then closed it and turned it over in his hands.

Kristin took it from him, slid the hidden key from a slot, then wound the mechanism. A haunting, old-fashioned melody began to play…an unnerving, awareness-building melody that captured the shop's cozy ambiance and heightened her awareness of the man beside her. She handed the box back to him.

"Pretty," he said.

"I think so, too."

Maybe the music was to blame for the moody shift in the air. Or maybe the shop was too warm. Or maybe old lovers with good memories shouldn't risk being alone in quiet places. Whatever the reason, Kristin felt herself grow jittery as the box continued to chime out a tender minuet, and the stirring smells of warm man and musky aftershave filled her nostrils.

He'd hurt her badly. Yet as her gaze fell from his eyes to his mouth, she was suddenly remembering kisses that tasted like sun-ripened strawberries and the smell of summer hay. Remembering the tingling touch of a boy who'd become a man in his aunt's hayloft…

Kristin reached out and slammed the lid, silencing the music and widening Zach's gray eyes. "That should give you some idea," she blurted, thankful she hadn't knocked the box out of his hands. "Actually, it's one of my favorite pieces—nineteenth century English sterling. Which also makes it very expensive."

Zach assessed her for a long beat, then glanced at the price tag and gave the box back to her. "I'll take it. Do you gift wrap?"

Surprise joined her flustered emotions. "Business must be good."

"I do all right."

Apparently so, she thought, moving to her register. She retrieved a gift box, tissue paper and ribbon from under the counter, suddenly all thumbs. What in the world was wrong with her? Chemistry again? Need? It had been a long time since she'd been with a man, but that was no reason to fall apart at the first sign of sexual interest.

She worked quickly, wanting to hurry, acutely aware of Zach's gaze on her. But pride wouldn't allow her to do a less-than-perfect job on the package. Finally, she was slipping it into a white bag printed with a watercolor of an old mill, annoyed with herself for wondering who would receive it.

She was about to take his credit card from the counter when Zach trapped her hand beneath his. It was warm, firm, and had her heart beating fast again. "Etta thinks we should talk," he said soberly. "She said we need 'closure.'"

The memory of that June night rushed back, crystal clear, wiping away those jittery feelings of awareness.

Kristin yanked her hand away, snared his credit card and started the transaction. It was amazing how easy it was to remain sensible when she recalled the pain, not the pleasure.

"Your aunt's a sweet woman, but maybe you should tell her that we've had closure for a long time." She handed him the receipt and a pen for his signature, waited for him to comply, then tossed his copy into the bag and handed it to him. "Now, I really do have to get busy."

If her shortness struck a chord in him, it didn't show.

"Me, too. The sooner I get Etta's house repaired and on the market, the sooner I can get back home."

Zach's inscrutable gaze moved over her face and hair, noted the small silver-and-turquoise posts in her earlobes, then slid down the front of her gray suit to her waist. "You look good, Kris," he said simply, meeting her eyes once more. Then without another word, he pushed away from the counter and walked out of her life again. Which suited Kristin just fine.

Chapter 3

At eight that evening, Kristin pulled her van into Anna Mae's driveway and parked beside a dark blue sedan. Angry voices drew her attention before she even shut off the engine. Sighing, she glanced through her open window. Her luck was certainly holding. Zach had made it a stressful day, and apparently, it was going to be a stressful night.

Standing beside a front lawn overrun by pinwheels, ceramic frogs, skunks and other lawn ornaments, Mildred Arnett and her middle-aged son were in the middle of an argument.

Kristin got out and slammed her door to alert them to her presence. But the short, plump woman with the Einstein frizz of hair and pink polyester pantsuit either didn't hear it or didn't care. Neither, it seemed, did her tall, heavyset son.

Will Arnett looked nothing like his mother. Where Mildred's complexion was powder-pale, Will's olive skin, thinning black hair and brushy mustache hinted at Greek or Italian ancestry. His khakis and yellow polo shirt looked expensive.

Dredging up a smile, Kristin called out a hello as she closed the distance between them. "Mrs. Arnett?"

Anna Mae's elderly cousin came forward and stretched out a hand. But as Kristin attempted to shake it, the woman slapped a set of keys into her palm. "Call me Mildred," she said, her sharp bird eyes taking in Kristin's white sweatshirt and jeans. "Just go on inside and do whatever it is that you do."

Kristin hesitated. "You aren't going with me?"

Will Arnett answered irritably, "Mother refuses to go inside Anna Mae's home after dark, and of course, it will be dark soon." He sent Kristin a deadpan expression and wiggled his fingers in the air. "Ghosts, you know."

Mildred scowled at her son, then spoke to Kristin. "I don't like thinking of Anna Mae dying in that house all alone, without someone to guide her spirit to the next level. I—I hear things in there." She cast a brief, nervous eye at the stately maples close to the house. "I've been trying to contact Ellysa all day, but I haven't been able to reach her. *She'd* know what the sounds mean."

Mildred seemed to expect a reply, so Kristin ventured, "Ellysa?"

Will rolled his eyes. "Ellysa Spectral, Mother's voodoo medium from the psychic hotli—"

"Ellysa is my *spiritual advisor*," Mildred cut in sharply.

"And she's draining your bank account. Every time you *consult* with her it's $5.95 a minute. What a colossal waste of money!"

"You'd know all about wasting money, wouldn't you? Maybe you should worry about getting a job instead of watching my bank balance!" Mildred swung a look at Kristin. "If there's anything you want to buy, let me know. I've already tagged the things I want. As I said on the phone, the rest will be auctioned off and the house put in the hands of a Realtor."

The mention of auctions brought back the compelling image of Zach in a tux, but Kristin quickly and determinedly chased it away. "Thank you for your trust. Shall I bring the keys to the motel when I've finished?"

"Yes, I'm in 103 and William's in 104—but bring the keys to *me*."

Kristin murmured her agreement, not daring to look at Will. "I'll see you in an hour or two. I'd like to take a good look."

"Whatever." Mildred jutted her chin skyward. "Come, William. I'd like to take a nap before that police show I like comes on the TV."

His face livid, Will Arnett nodded curtly at Kristin, then seated his mother in the blue sedan. She could hear them starting up again as they backed out of the driveway and roared off.

Kristin blew out a ragged breath. Chad hadn't exaggerated. They really were a strange twosome.

Not surprisingly, the inside of Anna Mae's house was clean, but cluttered—primarily because the rooms were small, but partly because the woman had been a pack rat. Downstairs, Kristin found several pots and vases that interested her, along with a bookcase full of classic literature, two of them, first editions. As Harlan had mentioned, frogs in all sizes were scattered from the kitchen to the upstairs bedrooms.

It was upstairs that she made her best finds, though the condition of the bedrooms disturbed her. The Arnetts hadn't taken much care as they'd gone through Anna Mae's things. Dresser drawers hung open, and most of the photos on the walls were askew. She tagged a pair of hurricane lamps and an old chest whose contents had also been tossed, then moved into the hallway to label a lovely old chair and occasional table before opening the door to the attic.

Several pairs of shoes sat just inside, and metal curtain rods that had never made it to the upper repository stood upright in the corner. Kristin snapped on the dim light and ascended the narrow staircase. She glanced around as she neared the top, smiling when she spied a dressmaker's dummy and several iron pipes hanging heavy with dated coats and dresses.

Suddenly glass smashed and the attic went dark. Kristin screamed as someone pushed past her and she tumbled midway down the stairs. She grasped for purchase, found the handrail, her mind on fire as footsteps banged down the remaining steps. The attic door slammed shut.

Afraid to move, afraid to breathe, Kristin crouched, nerves rioting, in the stairwell.

Something banged and bumped in the hall. Terrified, she backpedaled her way up several steps. She drew a trembling breath. He was moving furniture.

The thin strip of light beneath the attic door went out.

Kristin's pulse hammered so loudly in her ears it was nearly impossible to pick out other sounds. But after several long minutes, she sensed that the intruder had gone. Could she leave now? Did she dare tiptoe from the stairwell and call the police? What if he came back? What if he thought she'd seen him—could recognize him—and came back for her?

Dear God, he had to have been inside the entire time she was tagging merchandise!

Kristin felt her way down the last few steps, then located the light switch and prayed that the intruder had merely turned the light off upstairs and the sound she'd heard hadn't been the bulb smashing. But it had been.

She tried the door. Her heart sank when she realized he must have wedged the antique chair under the knob.

Frantic now, she pushed against it, shoved and pushed again—reared back and put her shoulder into it, banging until her arm ached. She dropped to the bottom step and thrust both feet against the door, again and again, harder, faster, harder.

Kristin screamed as the vibration sent a shower of curtain rods clattering down on her head.

They were a godsend.

Quickly, she maneuvered one of the flat metal rods under the door and rammed it hard against a chair leg. The chair flew out from under the knob and fell to the floor. Kristin burst into the hallway, fumbled shakily for the light switch, then raced downstairs and out of the house to use her car phone.

Patrolman Larry McIntyre was on the scene in less than five minutes, sirens wailing and lights flashing. After taking Kristin's statement and asking if she needed medical attention, he disappeared inside Anna Mae's little colonial home. Kristin was still sitting in her van when more headlights pierced the darkness and Chad brought his truck to a skidding stop behind the prowl car. He was in "civvies"—a gray sweatshirt bearing a police academy emblem, jeans and sneakers.

"What happened?" he asked tensely as he hurried to her open window. Lights strobed over his face. "Are you all right? I heard the call as I was getting out of the shower."

"I'm okay," she said with more confidence than she felt. "I'll probably have a few bruises from my graceful tumble down the steps, but I'm fine." Although, now that the crazy adrenaline rush had ceased, she was aware that her shoulder ached, and her right cheekbone felt tender.

"Thank God. Did you get a look at the guy?"

"No. To be honest, I can't even say for sure that it was a man. Everything happened too fast." She paused. "Larry thinks someone read the obituaries and decided to help himself while the house was still empty. He said he wouldn't be surprised if whoever broke in was looking for valuables to sell for drug money."

A deep scowl marred Chad's features. "We can't know that for sure, but it's possible. We're close enough to a major city to have our share of problems."

Kristin understood his anger. Everyone had their own causes. For Chad, it was drugs. From the day he'd apprehended a bucket-toting drug dealer collecting money for Anti-Drug Education outside a supermarket, that had been Chad's focus. Now he was tireless in his fight, speaking annually to school kids about the dangers of drug use. He believed that if he could reach them before the dealers did, they had a better chance of staying clean. He was still angry that a recent sting by state and tri-county police departments had failed because someone warned the dealers they were coming. Someone with inside information.

Chad sighed and looked toward the house. "Will you be okay while I see if Larry's come up with anything?"

"I'll be fine. Do your job."

"You're sure?" he said backing away.

"I'm sure. Go."

Kristin stared after him, wishing she could feel more than friendship for him. He truly did care about the town he protected and served. No one she knew would dispute that. At the same time, occasionally he did things that made her feel less kindly disposed to him. He was her friend. But he never passed up an opportunity to be photographed for the papers. Being a prime player in a major drug bust would've been a huge feather in his cap.

Minutes later, the lights went out in Anna Mae's home except for a lamp in the front window, and the two men came back out. With a wave, Larry climbed inside the prowl car, turned off the strobing lights and left. She'd given Larry the keys to Anna Mae's house when he arrived. Now Chad handed them back to her.

"I phoned the Arnetts," he said. "It's obvious from the splintering along the door frame that someone gained entry through the kitchen—probably after 5:00 p.m. and before eight o'clock when the Arnetts met you here. Mrs. Arnett's coming by tomorrow to see if anything's missing."

Chad paused, staring at the keys she held. "Why don't you let me return those for you? You should go home and rest."

"Thanks, but I can do it."

"I'd rather you didn't."

She smiled. "Don't hover."

A ragged sigh escaped him. "Okay, then I'll help Larry knock on some doors—see if the neighbors saw anyone hanging around here tonight. To be honest, I suspect he's long gone, but…that's the job." Chad's gaze softened, and he reached inside to touch her hair.

It made her a little sad. "Chad…"

"Yeah, I know," he murmured. "But if you ever change your mind, I could give you a good life." He smiled. "And we'd have great-looking kids."

"Thanks for coming by," was all she could say. Then he stepped away from the car and Kristin backed out of the driveway, wondering if the day would ever end.

The Wisdom Inn was a one-story, U-shaped series of units that opened directly onto a courtyard. It didn't have a presidential suite, but it was clean, well kept and, according to the neon sign near the road, offered a continental breakfast. But, Kristin thought as she walked in the cool darkness up to unit 103, she'd never stay here, particularly after tonight. Spotty, outdoor lighting and a door chain wasn't her idea of security.

She cringed as harsh words came through 103's wooden door.

"Ellysa *knew* something terrible would happen tonight!" Mildred shouted. "She says the person who broke in is someone I know."

"Oh yes, Mother," Will bellowed dramatically. "The great and powerful Ellysa Spectral knows all."

"She knows plenty. Where did *you* go while I napped tonight?"

Feeling herself pale, Kristin knocked loudly while

Mildred continued to rail at her son. It couldn't have been Will Arnett who'd knocked her down those stairs tonight, could it? How could he have entered the house and made his way to the attic without her knowledge? More to the point, why would he take a chance like that?

Will yanked open the door and greeted her wearily. "Hello, Ms. Chase."

"Hello. I'm just dropping off the—"

"Yes, I know, the keys. I'm so sorry for the trouble you ran into tonight. Is there anything we can do? Offer you some tea—a glass of wine, perhaps?"

Not in this lifetime. The last thing she needed was a drink at ringside. "That's very kind of you, but I need to get home. Chief Hollister said that you and your mother were coming by to check the house in the morning. Would you mind if I met you there again? I'd still like to look through the attic."

Mildred pushed forward, elbowing her son out of the way. "How about ten o'clock? I like to sleep in."

Kristin felt a faint smile form on her lips. There was no "How are you dear?" from the strange little woman, no apologies for the scare she'd experienced tonight. "Ten o'clock will be fine," Kristin said, backing away. "I'll see you at the house."

"Take care," Will said tiredly.

"You, too," she replied, meaning it. He probably needed all the care he could beg, borrow or steal to deal with his mother.

She couldn't imagine living in such an explosive household. She'd grown up in a warm, loving home with warm, loving parents who treated each other and their children with respect. Nothing like the behavior she'd seen from the Arnetts. Even in the last days of her life, Lillian Chase had never stopped smiling and encouraging her daughters. And Kristin had never stopped missing the father she'd lost in a car accident five years earlier.

"Kris?" A deep, familiar male voice called her name over the sound of dispensing ice. From Zach's tone, he was as surprised by their meeting as she was.

Kristin turned reluctantly toward the brightly lit alcove housing the soft drink machines. Dark sweatpants rode low on his hips, and the matching sweatshirt he wore was unzipped and hanging open. He was barefoot.

"Looking for me?" he asked, grinning faintly as he came forward. It was the closest he'd come to smiling since he'd returned—at least in his dealings with her—and for some ridiculous reason, that pleased her.

"No, I was returning Anna Mae's keys to Mrs. Arnett." Kristin kept her eyes above the dark, springy hair covering his chest. Thirteen years ago, only a strip of soft down had bisected his breastbone. "I thought you'd be staying at the farmhouse."

"I will be as soon as the water and power are turned back on. How did it go at Anna Mae's? Did you find some pieces for your shop?"

"A few. I was…I was interrupted and had to stop for a while. I'm going back tomorrow after church."

Zach ambled closer.

Kristin glanced toward the office where her car was parked, nerves skittering beneath her skin. His thick black hair was wet, and a soapy fragrance wafted on the night air. He kept his voice low in deference to the hour.

"I passed the church we used to go to on my way

back to the farmhouse last night. Hasn't changed mu—"

Suddenly, his face went slack, and he set the ice bucket down. "What happened to you?"

"Nothing," she replied, startled.

Reaching out, he turned her face toward the light. "Nothing? Your cheek's swollen and there's blood in your hair. Who did this?"

Blood? "No one. I fell."

"Come on." Grabbing her hand, he tugged her toward a unit several feet away. She cried out softly when the action jarred her aching shoulder.

Zach's gaze hardened. "You fell?"

"I'm fine."

"All right, you're fine. Don't tell me what happened. And don't accept my help. But if you don't get some ice on your cheek pretty damn soon, you're going to look like a poster girl for domestic abuse."

"All right!" Striding through the door, she moved past the disheveled bed with the plain blue coverlet, and entered his tiny bathroom. It seemed even smaller with shower mist and the intimate smells of soap and shampoo still hanging in the air. Butterflies battered her stomach as Zach reached past her to wipe the steam from the mirror, then stood behind her, staring at their reflections.

Kristin sighed. Blood was caked near her temple, and there was a reddish-blue bruise on her cheekbone.

Zach grabbed a washcloth, dropped some ice into it, then put the pack in her hand. "Now," he said gravely. "What went on tonight?"

She told him. He wasn't much happier when she finished.

"Chad didn't insist that you get checked out at the

hospital? And why in hell didn't *he* deliver the keys to the Arnetts so you could go home and take care of yourself? Or didn't he even notice that you'd been hurt?''

"Zach, please," she said, pressing the ice pack to her face. "I'm tired, and I don't feel like defending Chad's actions to you tonight. He did offer, but I refused. It was more important that he investigate the break-in. As for his not noticing, I was sitting in the dark, and my right side was turned away from him.''

"You were standing in a dark courtyard and *I* noticed."

She shook her head. This was a mistake. She should never have let him bully her into coming in here. When he made sounds like a man who cared, it was too easy to forget that he'd nearly destroyed her, and too easy to remember that they'd once owned each other's souls.

"I need to go," she said, shoving the ice pack in his hands. "Thank you."

"Wait. I want to see something." Dropping the pack into the sink, he moved closer and turned her face up to his. After the ice, his hand was warm against her skin, and tiny nerve endings responded. "It's still red," he said quietly.

"Makeup will cover it."

"Will it?"

"Yes, I'm sure it—" She stiffened. "What are you doing? Zach—?"

Warm breath fanned the hair at her temple as his lips brushed her cheekbone. "Just kissing it to make it better."

Kristin rammed both palms into his chest and

shoved him away. "How dare you?" she demanded shakily, more furious with herself for allowing the kiss than she was with him. "You gave up the right to do that the night you slept with Gretchen Wilder."

Chapter 4

Zach's gray eyes churned angrily as he looked down at her. He was a big man, and even the full force of her shove wasn't enough to do more than shift his stance.

He reached for her shoulders, then suddenly seemed to remember her injury and backed off. But he was still so close, she could feel the heat of his body, could count every black whisker in his day-old beard, every eyelash fringing his accusing gaze.

"Still throwing all the blame in my lap? Well, you know what I think? I think you were glad I slept with Gretchen. No, not glad—*ecstatic*. It saved you from manufacturing even more reasons why you couldn't marry me."

Kristin bolted through the doorway, her sneakers punishing the walk as he followed her out. "I never manufactured anything. Everything I said was true."

"Like hell! You never told me how sick your mother was!"

She whirled to face him. "The news was too new. I couldn't. Not until *you* broke off our relationship. Then I realized that no matter how deeply into denial I was—no matter how frightened I was that saying the word 'terminal' would make it true—I had to tell you the truth before I lost you, too. And when I finally found the courage to say that word, where were you? Lying in the weeds with Gretchen. Four hours, Zach! Four lousy hours away from me, and you were making love to someone else!"

Nearby streetlights threw his face into bold relief, anger still burning in his eyes. "I didn't make love to her, I had sex with her. They're two different things."

"Oh, yes, let's split hairs."

"I told you how sorry I was. It meant nothing!"

"It meant everything! It meant I had no one to hold me and help me through her illness! It meant I could never trust you again."

Kristin brought her lips together, suddenly aware that their shouts were echoing in the courtyard. They had to stop before they had an audience, if people weren't already peeping through the cracks in their drapes. She lowered her voice, and it trembled as she struggled for control. "Never mind, it doesn't matter anymore."

"It does matter, or you wouldn't have brought it up." Zach lowered his voice, too. "You knew how insecure I was about you. You knew about my life and my past, and you knew that a long string of excuses not to marry me would make me doubt your feelings."

"*What* string of excuses?"

"First, you were afraid I'd always be on the road

and you'd be alone in unfamiliar surroundings. When I told you I'd be working with the permanent crew in Durham, it barely made a difference. Then it was the scholarship that stood in the way, even though I told you we'd find a way to pay for your out-of-state schooling. By the time you told me that you were refusing the scholarship to stay with your mom, why wouldn't I have had doubts? Especially when you let me think she was going to get better. When you couldn't even look at me that day, I thought I had my answer, and it was no. No marriage, no me and you." He expelled an impatient breath. "*That's* why Gretchen happened."

Kristin's voice shook. "Don't you dare try to justify what you did. Gretchen 'happened' because you *let* it happen. I'm sorry you had a lousy life. But I didn't have time to wonder that day if what I said was what you heard." Her voice broke. "My mother was dying, and there was nothing I could do to stop it."

The night stilled around them, every molecule frozen in time and space as her words hung heavy in the air. For several very long seconds, neither of them moved, the hum of tires on the highway punctuating the long silence.

"If I'd known that," he said finally, "things would've been different."

Instead of making her feel better, his reply hurt her all over again. If he'd really loved her and thought their relationship was over, he would have been too devastated to *want* anyone else. That's how she'd felt. Instead, he'd made love to his free-spirited, easy neighbor while Kristin was reeling from their breakup and trying to come to grips with her mother's cancer. She'd had to handle it all without him. And she'd needed him more desperately then than she'd ever needed anyone or anything since.

Turning away, she headed toward the neon sign near the office where her van was parked.

Zach didn't try to stop her, and she didn't look back.

He did get in the last cold words. "I told you how sorry I was the night it happened and again at your mother's funeral. I phoned you and wrote letters that came back unopened. I'm through groveling, Kris."

Kristin managed to cling to her anger and keep her tears at bay until she pulled into the concrete drive beside her town house and entered her apartment. Then there was no holding back.

Dammit, she thought as the tears fell. She wasn't responsible for their breakup! *He* was. His immaturity—not his insecurity—was to blame. And after thirteen years, why did she still care what he thought or didn't think?

But minutes later as she stood in the kitchen holding more ice to her cheek, the scene outside Zach's motel room came back to her.

Was there a kernel of truth in what he'd said? Had she, unknowingly, been looking for excuses to put off their wedding?

She'd been completely devoted to him—no one could tell her that she hadn't been. But at eighteen, *had* she been ready to leave her home and family to start a new life in a new state? Could she have been making excuses that she wasn't even aware of?

Kristin threw the ice into the sink and heated water for tea. The hold he still had on her was incomprehensible. Tonight, she'd been shoved down half a

flight of steps, locked in an attic stairwell and frightened to the soles of her feet.

And still, all she could think of was Zach.

Zach jerked open his briefcase on the bed, shuffled
through the copies of the strip mall estimates he'd
brought along with him, then dropped to the bedspread
and picked up the phone again. He cradled the receiver
on his shoulder while he located the specs for the
space they were converting to a popular toy franchise.

"Okay, Dan, I'm looking at the floor plan now,"
he said to his foreman. "And yeah, that half wall has
to come down. You know the drill. All the stores in
the franchise have to look alike for easy shopping."

"Can't get even a little creative?"

"We save our creativity for the beach houses."

"Fine by me, just thought I'd ask before we ripped
it down." He paused, his Carolina drawl growing
slightly curious. "Things goin' okay there? You don't
sound happy."

"I'm so happy, I'm damn-near delirious," he
growled sarcastically. "It shouldn't take me more than
two weeks to finish here, then I'll be home. In the
meantime, call if you run into any problems, and I'll
continue to phone you daily for updates. Is the other
crew ready to start the Hart's beach house?"

"Day after tomorrow."

"Good. Tell them to take special care with this one.
Mrs. Hart has a lot of rich, influential friends. We want
her endorsement."

"They take special care on all the jobs," Dan returned, chuckling. "They don't want to end up in the
unemployment line. Talk to you tomorrow."

Zach hung up the phone, his nerves still thrumming.

He'd told Kristin he wouldn't grovel and he meant it. So why couldn't he just put her out of his mind and go to sleep?

Grabbing some change from the top of the dresser, he went outside, then crossed the courtyard to the vending machines and bought another Pepsi. Angry voices came from a nearby unit, but he didn't give a damn about their problems. He had enough of his own. He took a long drink and started back to his room.

He'd been acting like an idiot since he hit town, and it was all because of her. First he'd let Chad needle him into some kind of pseudo-high school rivalry, then he'd lost his focus and kissed Kris. He took another long swallow.

She was wrong, blaming him for all of it. If what she'd felt for him was love, she couldn't have kept quiet about her mother's illness. Not even for a minute. She would've needed to tell him—needed for him to hold her and tell her things would be all right. Instead…

Instead, Gretchen found him behind Etta's barn that night, working on his second six-pack and wondering why his father thought booze could ease a man's pain. And that time when she offered a different kind of remedy, he didn't say no.

Crumpling the empty can, Zach went inside where the air conditioner was finally clearing away the shower mist, and tossed it into the wastebasket beside the bureau. It clattered against hard plastic.

All right, he thought, going to the bed and repacking his briefcase. He'd been a bastard. That was old news. But Kris wasn't completely faultless. She'd known how insecure he was about her feelings, especially with Hollister champing at the bit to take her away. She should've told him the whole truth.

Stripping to his briefs, he flopped down on the bed, then grabbed the remote control from the nightstand and hit the on button. In a burst of color and canned laughter, the set sprang to life.

Tender kisses in motel rooms were for him and some other woman now—some other *temporary* woman. He didn't have time to worry about old relationships or start new ones. He had a company to run, an empire to build. At thirty-three, he was finally earning respect and position, things that had been denied him from birth, and nothing was going to get in the way of that. His business was his chief priority. He didn't need Kristin Chase in his life anymore.

Two days later, Zach grabbed a towel, swiped the sawdust and sweat from his arms and chest, then sank to the top step of Etta's front porch and snatched up his cell phone. He frowned as indecision gripped him again. Then he swore and dialed Kristin's number from memory. Overhead, the Monday afternoon sun beat down through the tall maples, relentless in its effort to burn every square inch of his exposed skin.

"Hi," he said soberly when she picked up the phone at her shop.

The long pause on her end had Zach wondering if she was trying to place his voice.

"This is a surprise," she said coolly.

He imagined it was, since they hadn't parted on the best of terms Saturday night. "I had some time, so I thought I'd call and see if your cheek was okay."

"It's fine."

"Your shoulder?"

"That's fine, too."

Zach reined in his impatience. All of her responses were tolerant and polite, but obviously, she was still angry. He damned the illogical compulsion that made him keep trying with her. "Any news on the intruder?" he asked, committed to make the best of it.

"Not yet, but I'm hoping Chad will have some information when he comes over later."

Considering his aversion to Hollister, the jealous pinch he experienced was hardly unexpected. "Going out for dinner?"

"No, before the Arnetts went home yesterday, I bought a few of Anna Mae's pieces and the contents of her attic. Half of it's being delivered this afternoon. Chad's helping me find room for it in my shop."

"Nice of him," Zach drawled.

"He *is* nice," she replied. "And if you were a little more flexible in your thinking, you'd be able to see that." She paused, and her tone softened. "I know he gave you a hard time in school. But he's not the same person he was then."

"Leopards don't change their spots."

"This one did."

Right. The kid who'd never shown a shred of compassion to anyone below him in the social pecking order, had turned over a new leaf. Zach wouldn't put money on it.

He'd been the son of the boozed-up school janitor—a job his dad was given only because Etta was on the school board and did some serious begging. Of course, her intervention hadn't worked. Though she'd hoped her nephew would straighten out and support his teenage son when they returned to Wisdom, Hap Davis was out of a job in four months, and dead of cirrhosis a year later.

"Zach?"

Zach yanked himself out of the past, annoyed that he'd made the trip. He hadn't allowed those thoughts into his mind for years. "I'm here," he said into the receiver. "Just hoping there's an arrest soon. You don't have to go back to that house, do you?"

"No. I'll have nearly everything I need by six o'clock tonight, and the rest will be here on Wednesday."

Everything she needed. He resisted the urge to ask if Hollister was part of that package. "Well, I'd better get back to work on Etta's porch." Pushing to his feet, he crossed to the fringe of grass near the driveway where his table saw was set up. "I'm glad you're okay," he finished gruffly.

"Thank you. I am, too. Goodbye, Zach."

"Bye."

Frowning, Zach set the phone aside, turned the saw back on, and went back to work cutting floorboards for Etta's porch. He was still keyed up and didn't know why. The feeling was really beginning to aggravate him.

Kristin hung up the phone and pressed a hand to her stomach, trying to quiet her butterflies.

All right…this is good, she decided, willing her heartbeat to slow, willing herself to breathe normally. They were speaking civilly. That would be helpful if they bumped into each other again before he went back home. And in a town the size of Wisdom, it was a near certainty.

Tamping down the rush of nerves that thought

evoked, she returned to her sales floor to ready it for
her new acquisitions.

Kristin shoved a table full of lace doilies and votive
cups closer to the wall, then carried a spinning wheel
to the front and set it near a wooden barrel topped
with potpourri. Standing back, she visually measured
the space she'd cleared near the door to her stockroom.
It wasn't big enough.

Anna Mae's attic had been pack-rat heaven, she
thought, determined to concentrate on the job at
hand—not the gray eyes that kept filling her mind.
There'd never be enough room to store everything
here in the shop. She needed to look into self-storage
places.

Three hours later, Kristin stood near the side door
and directed Chad and a deliveryman named Wayne
where to stack the merchandise from Anna Mae's
home. In the dim light, it had been difficult to assess
the worth of some of those attic pieces. Now she could
see that she'd bargained well with the Arnetts. Some
of the items were absolutely lovely—a fact that was
totally lost on the heavy, middle-aged deliveryman
with the ponytail, tattoos and multistudded earlobes.

He'd already dropped a carton of books and it had
split open in the paved alley between her shop and
Harlan's tax office. She stepped back from the door
as Chad carried an antique chair inside from the wide
alley.

"Where do you want this?" His tone turned dry.
"Is there room behind the cash register where *Wayne*
put the books he dropped?"

She lowered her voice as she followed him inside.
"Yes, just set it there. And thanks for helping. Espe-

cially since he's not the most cautious person on the planet.''

"That's an understatement. If there'd been breakables in that box you would have lost them all.''

Kristin put a fingertip to her lips as the deliveryman came back inside with another load. Only his boots and faded jeans were visible beneath a tall stack of boxes.

"I'll tell him again to watch what he's doing,'' Chad muttered.

"No, don't make waves. Nothing's been damaged. There can't be that much more to— Oh, no,'' she groaned looking at one of the marked cartons. "He has glass this time.'' And the boxes were piled so high, he could barely see around them.

Kristin hurried forward to take the top box from him, but Chad beat her to it.

"Buddy,'' he said coldly as he snatched it away. "This lady's going to give you the tongue lashing of your life if you drop one more thi—'' Chad went stone still.

Because it was Zach's face, not the deliveryman's, behind the box.

A whisper of a smile touched Zach's lips as he settled his gaze on Kristin. "In that case, maybe I should drop something on purpose.''

Fighting an embarrassed flush, she found her voice before Chad could start an argument. "I—I thought you were working on Etta's porch.''

"I was, but I wanted to get to the mall before it closed. Now that the power is back on and I'm staying at the house, I decided to buy one of those cheap spongy futons. Etta's hardwood floors aren't the most comfortable.''

"No, I suppose they aren't," Kristin returned. Above those boots and faded jeans, he wore a navy blue T-shirt that hugged his shoulders and chest. And though it wasn't fair to compare the two men, next to Chad's fair skin and clean-shaven blondness, Zach was darkly intriguing.

He spoke again. "I saw the truck and remembered you said you were expecting a delivery today. Thought I'd give you a hand."

Chad sent him a chilling look. "I've already given her both of mine. If you have work to do, feel free to get back to it."

"Nah, I've been at it most of the day. I'll just grab a few more boxes. The guy in the truck was shuffling them from the back to the tailgate so they'd be easier to unload. He's probably finished by now."

Zach smiled. "Want to bring both of your hands outside, Hollister? We can probably finish unloading the rest in just a few minutes."

Chad's face turned a deeper shade of crimson. He didn't like being mocked, and it showed. "I intended to," he said coldly, obviously trying to snatch back a little power. "Just watch your step carrying those boxes in here."

Ten minutes later, the tension increased markedly when the deliveryman drove off, leaving the three of them alone. Between her taut nerves, Zach's presence and Chad's brooding silence, Kristin was so wired, it was difficult to keep her mind on arranging the new merchandise in the best possible order.

Zach's deep voice carried to her from the front of the store where he was inventorying cartons and scrawling a list of contents on the sides of the boxes. "Your shop looks good, Kris."

"Oh, it's lovely," she joked nervously, hoisting the broken box of books from the floor to the counter. "You must be a big fan of clutter."

"I wasn't talking about the clutter. I was talking about the changes you've made. It used to be a major tourist trap."

Yes, it had been. Amish buggy key-chains, tiny cedar outhouses and cheap cardboard hex signs had abounded. But when Marian Grant put it up for sale seven years ago, it was exactly what Kristin had been looking for. She'd loved the prime location where faux Victorian gaslights lit the street and spills of petunias hung from double holders on the parking meters— where the bakery across the street filled the air with mouthwatering smells and Eli Elliott's coffee bar and country bookstore drew patrons from all over. The street was so quaint, so warm and charming, that she knew it was the ideal place for the shop she wanted to open.

"You have good taste," Zach finished.

"Thank you. I try."

Chad sidled up to her as she delved into the small carton of first editions. Their hands tangled and their bodies brushed as he reached inside to help. Kristin inched away, feeling even more awkward.

"Actually, I think her taste has improved a lot over the years," Chad remarked.

"How's that?" Zach called.

"Oh, the company she keeps, for one thing. She hangs out with a classier group of people now."

"Really?" Zach asked with a slow smile. "Compared to whom?"

Kristin glared at Chad, then fumbled with the books, feeling the temperature in the room rise. He and Zach were headed for a confrontation, sure as heat in July, and she had to diffuse it. "Chad, could you grab a—"

She'd intended to ask for a sturdier box in which to store the books. But as the words left her mouth, the other side of the damaged box split open and books tumbled from the glass counter and fell to the floor. With an exasperated sigh, she dropped to her knees to close the books that had opened before their pages could be creased and ruined.

Suddenly she halted, seeing three volumes that shouldn't have been included in the shipment. "I didn't tag these," she said quizzically. "Someone must have put them in the box by mistake."

Chad knelt beside her. "What are they?"

"Anna Mae's journals." Frowning, Kristin examined them closely. "I suppose it was an easy mistake to make. All of the books are leather bound and similar in size."

"Well, obviously you can't sell them," Chad replied, taking them from her. "I'll put them over there with the things for the Dumpster."

Kristin sprang to her feet and took the journals back, startled that he'd even consider such a thing. It was like throwing away a life. "No, don't do that." She placed them on the counter near her cash register. "I have Mrs. Arnett's phone number in my office. She'd probably love to have them."

"Oh. Right," he said, with a shrug. "I didn't think of that."

A rap at the shop's etched glass door drew their attention, and Councilman Len Rogers opened the door a crack and poked his head in.

"Evening," he called.

Smiling, Kristin waved him inside. "Hi, Len. I'm

closed, but if there's something in particular that you need you're welcome to look around.''

"Actually, I just need to see the chief for a moment," he replied with a warm smile of his own.

"Sure. Come on back. Just watch the cartons strewn all over the place.''

Rogers hesitated, glanced at the envelope in his hand and said, ''Actually, it's business. Can we speak in private, Chad?''

"Sure." Chad wended his way through the cartons, then followed Rogers outside. A few minutes later, he came back in. "Kristin, I'm sorry, but one of my men came by while I was outside talking to Len. I need to drive up to York and see a colleague."

"Oh?"

"Yeah." He hesitated, then said, "Bill Schrecongost. Bill was one of the officers involved in May's drug roundup. He has information that might lead us to the informant who blew the whistle." He met her eyes apologetically. "See you tomorrow?"

"Sure. Thanks for helping out. I'll buy the coffee."

"Uh-uh, that's my job. We wouldn't want to break tradition." Then, with another glare at Zach, he left.

The sound of the door closing was like a rifle shot, firing adrenaline to every cell in Kristin's body. It also seemed to act as a summons because as Chad left, Zach walked toward her. The bottom fell out of her stomach.

"All finished marking the cartons?" she asked to cover her jitters.

"I've been finished. Thought I'd give you some quality time with lover boy without interrupting." His voice dropped. "Actually, now that he's gone, we can talk."

"About what?" she asked warily.

"Something Chad mentioned earlier."

"Again, what?"

Zach's hooded gaze stroked hers, and the masculine scents of warm man and musky attraction started Kristin's pulse racing.

"The tongue lashing of my life," he murmured. "Why don't we talk about that?"

Chapter 5

Kristin's weak-kneed feeling fled in a rush of annoyance. "Don't start, Zach."

He grinned. "Sorry, couldn't resist."

"Try."

Shrugging, he reached past her to take the journals from the showcase, glanced at the dates on the front, then frowned and set them aside. "I agree that these shouldn't be thrown away. But I also think Anna Mae's private thoughts should remain private."

He met her eyes. "How would you feel if someone read *your* diaries? Learned intimate details you'd written down because they were too personal to share with anyone?"

Kristin's jitters came stealing back. She hadn't had reason to record anything of that nature since she was seventeen and Zach's lover. There'd been nothing remarkable about the few relationships she'd had since then.

Moving away, she grabbed an empty box in which to store the literature collection. "First of all," she said, returning to transfer the books. "I don't keep a diary."

"Nothing intimate to report?" he asked in an amused tone. "Hollister's not keeping you happy? I noticed he didn't kiss you goodbye."

Kristin sent him a withering look. "Who I kiss or don't kiss is none of your business. Getting back to your question about my keeping a diary, I don't have the time or the inclination to jot down anything more involved than a shopping list these days. However, I believe that people who do keep journals write to be read—to give their lives importance and recognition. Whether you know it or not, Anna Mae was an extraordinary woman. Chad said she was a Peace Corps volunteer when she was younger."

"I knew she was a good woman," Zach said. "I didn't know about the Peace Corps thing."

"You knew her well enough to know she was 'good'?"

His gaze clouded. "When your dad's dragged into the police station on drunk and disorderly charges every time the moon changes, you get to know a lot of people who work there."

"Oh." Sorry she'd asked, Kristin averted her eyes and moved the conversation away from that hurtful time in his life. "You weren't the only one who didn't know about Anna Mae being a volunteer. I didn't either. In fact, I doubt many people did."

"That tells me that she valued her privacy. It also tells me she might not want people poking around in her diaries."

Kristin paused, her hands resting on the carton. "We're not going to agree on this, are we?"

"No, probably not. Feels like a trend, doesn't it?" That reminder of their past had him taking in her sleeveless white blouse and beige skirt, and suddenly Kristin wished she hadn't removed her matching jacket.

Lifting the box, she moved away from the counter and headed for her open stockroom door. Zach intercepted her on the way.

"Here—let me get that," he said, taking it from her.

Kristin stilled as his fingertips brushed her blouse just below her breasts in the process.

"Where do you want this?"

"Anywhere you can find a space," she answered, pretending she hadn't felt the contact. "It's getting crowded in there." And it was getting warm out here.

Zach went inside, shuffled some things around, then poked his head out again. "If I rearrange some things, there'll be room for those cartons I marked, too. Do you want them back here?"

No, she just wanted *him* out of her shop. He was getting to her again, and she didn't like the vulnerable feeling it gave her. "Thanks, but I'll get them in the morning. Let's just call it a night."

He sent her a tolerant look. "Are you sure? Some of them have to weigh fifty pounds."

Kristin nodded and hid a sigh. It was ridiculous to refuse his help. "Thank you. I'll just get my jacket and the day's receipts from my office and be right back."

Moving inside, she pulled on her jacket, stuffed the night deposit bag into her purse and picked up a stack of paperwork she hadn't completed. Then she returned to the storefront and set everything beside the cash register.

She grew increasingly anxious listening to the sounds of boxes being dragged across the tile floor and being lifted and thumped down, presumably, one on top of the other. The longer they spent together, the more those old memories and feelings came back.

Finally, he emerged, dusting his hands on his jeans. "That about it?"

"Yes," she answered in relief. "Thanks again. You go on ahead. I just have to turn off the lights and lock up."

"I'm not in any hurry," he said, to her chagrin. "I'll wait and walk you out."

Sighing, Kristin returned to her office. In a moment, she was back out, having turned off everything except the lights in the bay window and a tiny lamp at the back of the store. Zach was beside the showcase. She slowed her steps as she realized something tense and imminent had gathered in his eyes. Something that made her hold her breath.

"Well," she said, striding around him to grab her purse, "as Scarlett O'Hara said, tomorrow's another day."

Zach caught her hand.

Kristin stopped breathing again as he moved closer, his gray eyes telegraphing his intent, and giving her ample time to refuse the kiss she knew was coming. Her heart banged against her rib cage as he slid his hands inside her open jacket and coaxed her to him.

Why wasn't she saying no? Why wasn't she pushing him away? Why wasn't she telling him that he had no right to touch her anymore?

She had no answers. Because she was suddenly too

involved in the texture and feel of him to care. Dear God, it had been so long since she'd felt like this. She'd been sure that a normal physical response was dead to her forever. And yet, here it was...that nervous quiver, that breathless tremble, that downward whoosh of the Ferris wheel.

Zach's gaze grew heavy lidded as he touched her cheek where makeup hid the bruise from her fall. Then instinct took over, memories took over, and they came together in a hard, hungry kiss that was an explosion of heat and hormones.

They drank wetly from each other, broke the kiss only to claim it again and delve more deeply. His tongue darted into her mouth and she took it greedily, and gave him hers.

Moments passed and that languid feeling of wanting to lie down overpowered her, while her mind floated and a tiny voice whispered that they'd be more comfortable on the floor. She could feel Zach's hand pressing against her bottom, feel the need to move against him in that slow, sensual dance that always brought back the smell of strawberries and freshly mown hay. And suddenly she was back in that old loft where she'd learned about passion for the very first time...where Zach's hands and kisses had—

Kristin pulled away in a panicky rush of self-preservation, then skittered back a few paces to give herself room to think. Because she couldn't think when he was this close. She didn't know how he did it, but when he was around, her mind shut down and her heart took over.

"We can't do this."

"Why not?" he murmured, his eyes still heavy lidded as he reached for her again. "Obviously, we still click."

Kristin sidestepped him, dismayed by his word choice and her lack of common sense. "I don't *want* to 'click' with you." She wanted to click with someone else, someone reliable, someone who wouldn't betray her when his insecurities flared. Someone who wouldn't be leaving again.

"It doesn't appear that either of us has a choice."

"We're adults. We always have a choice." Moving to the glass showcase, she picked up her purse and paperwork and started toward the door, her nerve ends still buzzing.

The hard truth was she'd wanted that kiss to happen since she'd seen him on the runway last Saturday night. Now that it had, it was more than she'd bargained for. She threw open the door to the warm night air. "Let's just chalk it up to curiosity and forget it."

"Can we forget it?" he asked, joining her outside and waiting for her to lock up.

"Why not? It's not as though it meant anything. I suspect that most people with a past like ours would be curious if they found themselves alone in a dimly lit room. But it can't happen again."

"Not even if we wanted it to?"

Kristin froze for an instant and looked at him wondering why he'd said that. "Not even." Then she turned to the right and strode to her van, parked in the tiny lot she shared with the tax office. Zach came with her and opened her door, then waited until she'd put her things on the passenger's seat before he spoke again.

"Be careful driving home," he said as she started the van. "It's a warm night. The deer will be out."

"I will. Thank you for your help."

"Thank you for the kiss."

Kristin sighed and shook her head. "Zach, what do you get out of constantly baiting me? It wasn't a gift. It was a mistake." Then shutting the door, she pulled out.

But unsettled as she was, she couldn't stop herself from watching in her rearview mirror as he walked to his truck and climbed behind the wheel.

Zach tossed and turned in his sleeping bag on the hardwood floor of his aunt's empty living room, fed up with the chirping of the crickets and peeper frogs beyond the window screens. He'd forgotten about the futon in his truck until he'd stripped to his underwear, and had decided to tough it out one more night. He'd forgotten about nearly everything but Kris. He could still smell her perfume.

He flipped his pillow to the cool side. He'd thought that sleep would erase her from his mind. But she'd been there in his dreams, too, and he'd awakened fully aroused and needy.

What a surprise she was. He'd known a young, naive girl. She was so much more than that now. She was beautiful and confident and strong and sexy. Good God, no wonder he couldn't sleep.

The cell phone beside him rang.

Zach swung a quick glance at his lighted travel alarm. The only reason for a call at one in the morning was trouble, and the only person he could imagine calling at this hour was his foreman.

He grabbed the phone. "Dan?"

"No, dear, it's me," Etta said, obviously worried. Zach clamped the phone between his cheek and shoulder, and snatched up his socks and jeans from the floor where he'd left them two hours ago. He spoke while he yanked them on. "Aunt Etta, what's wrong?"

"I'm all right, honey, but Kristin's in trouble."

A second jolt of adrenaline hit him. *Had there been another break-in? Had the person who'd shoved her down Anna Mae's attic stairs meant to hurt her?* "What happened? Is she all right?"

"As far as I know, she's not hurt, but it just came over my scanner that her shop is on fire. The sirens are still going full blast."

Zach thanked heaven for his aunt's nosy streak. A full quarter of the residents in her senior building had scanners and relentlessly monitored the police channel. "Did they say how many units were dispatched?"

"No, but Lancaster's answering, too."

Zach tugged on his boots, then rose to flip on the lights and dig a wrinkled-but-clean black T-shirt from his duffel bag.

"I thought you'd want to know," Etta went on. "I imagine she's at the fire."

"I'm leaving right now. Thanks for calling."

"Tell her if there's anything I can do—"

"I will. Love you. Bye." Then he doused the lights and carried his phone to his truck. He could hear sirens in the distance now, smell the faint, but unmistakable stench of smoke on the air.

Zach's gut clenched and his heart followed suit as old guilt settled heavily on his shoulders. She'd needed him when her mother was dying, and he hadn't been there. He'd be there for her now.

Ten minutes later, Zach squealed into the paved lot beside old Eli Elliott's bookstore and came to a stop next to Kristin's van. Eli's store was built on a slight knoll above and across the street from her shop, giving Zach a bird's-eye view of the blaze. His heart sank at the number of fire trucks, emergency vehicles and utility workers on the scene.

Everyone was moving and yelling, but the fire leapt and roared, creating its own wind, eating everything Kristin had worked so hard to build. She had to be devastated. Smoke and ash billowed from her smashed bay window, and on both sides of her shop, firefighters hosed down the adjacent buildings in an attempt to prevent the fire from spreading.

Searching the scene, he spotted her standing some distance away near a barricade of sawbucks and yellow police tape. Zach hurried down the grassy embankment to the street. Arms hugging herself, she was speaking with councilman Len Rogers, Harlan Greene, Eli and another man he didn't recognize.

He stopped ten yards away from them to gauge her reaction—to see if he'd be welcomed or run off. When she murmured a few words to her friends and trudged slowly toward him, he had his answer. He could feel the heat of the fire now, see its orange reflection on her face. The pain in her eyes almost crushed him. Then she was walking into his open arms, letting him hold her, and pressing her forehead to his shoulder.

She didn't stay there long. After a few moments and a deep breath, she pulled herself together and eased away from him. She nodded toward the wrought-iron benches between Eli's bookstore and the bakery. "Let's sit."

When they were seated, she turned to him, her eyes damp and her expression bleak. "How did you know?"

"Etta. She heard it on her scanner. She said to call if there's anything she can do for you."

She looked at him wearily. "I can't think of what that might be right now."

"Come here," he murmured and tried to draw her close again.

She eased his hands away. "I can't." The glare from the fire flickered over her lined face. "I'm only holding it together by a thread, and if I let you hold me again, you're going to get wet."

"I can handle it."

"But I can't. If I let myself cry, I won't be able to stop."

"Okay," he answered, needing to do *something* for her. "Can I hold your hand, at least?"

She blinked several times, then put her hand in his. She squeezed so hard he thought she'd shut off his circulation.

"How did it happen?"

Kristin shook her head. "I don't know. Len said he thought it started in the rear of the shop. He's the one who turned in the alarm. He was leaving the Elks' club and saw the smoke."

She drew a trembling breath. "Zach, I've been wracking my brain, trying to come up with a reason for this, and I just can't. I'm careful. I don't keep oily rags or combustible chemicals around. I'm cautious to the point of being compulsive about fire hazards. I never leave the shop *or* my apartment without making certain everything's in order."

But a tiny, contradicting fear had crept in while she was speaking. Yes, usually she was cautious. But last night, she hadn't been thinking clearly because Zach was in the shop—because of that kiss. Maybe in her haste to lock up, she'd somehow overlooked something. Had she hit a breaker she shouldn't have touched when she shut off the lights? But, no. Shutting off breakers didn't start electrical fires.

Another possibility occurred to her, and her spirits sank lower. "I don't store chemicals in my shop…but Zach, I didn't open all of the boxes from Anna Mae's attic. What if there was something combustible in one of them?"

"That's pretty remote," he said quietly. "The people who packed up your things wouldn't have shipped something like that."

"I didn't tag Anna Mae's diaries either, but they showed up, didn't they?" She massaged the ache over her eyes. "Dammit, why didn't I take the time to look through all of the cartons?"

"Because you're not superwoman. There had to be forty or fifty boxes in that delivery and it was after eight o'clock when you got it all inside. No one would have had the time to look."

She didn't know if he was right or not, but even if he was paying her lip service, it was comforting.

"Here comes someone," Zach said, with a nod toward the grass embankment.

Kristin's heart leapt as Captain Williams trudged toward them, backlit by smoke and flames, his hat and face mask gone, his long yellow slicker hanging open. She stood quickly, and Zach followed suit. Soot blackened the fireman's cheeks, and his rumpled hair clung damply to his forehead.

Any hope she still had fled because there was none on Williams's face.

"Ma'am, I'm afraid it looks like a total loss," he said. "We got here as quick as we could, but we're a volunteer fire department. By the time we drive to the hall, get the trucks and make it to the scene, the fire's already got a good start.'' He glanced back at her shop. ''I'm afraid wood structures go up fast. A few things in the front of your store might've withstood the heat, but then you've got smoke and water damage to contend with.''

Tears stung her eyes. ''Do you have any idea yet what caused it?''

''No, ma'am. That'll be up to the fire marshal to determine.''

''I see. How soon will he be investigating?'' She was aware of Zach behind her, gently massaging her shoulder. She clutched his hand. ''Is he down there now?''

''No, I'm sorry. He's out of town. In Pennsylvania, fire marshals are trained state police officers, and there aren't that many of them. Ours has a pretty big district to cover. It could be three days to a week 'til he gets here.''

He nodded at the blaze. It was slowly coming under control. ''We'll hang around until we're sure there are no more hot spots. We'll also post volunteer fire police outside to make sure no one enters or disturbs the scene 'til the marshal makes his determination.'' Williams paused. ''I'm afraid that means you, too, Ms. Chase.''

''Of course,'' Kristin answered. ''Thank you. My—my thanks to all of you.''

Still fighting tears, she watched him leave. Then she turned to Zach and swallowed the lump in her throat. ''At least they saved Harlan's office and Ben's shop.''

He nodded grimly. ''I know I don't have to ask this, but you were insured, right?''

"Yes. Probably overinsured. But two-thirds of everything I had in the shop came from another era. They can never be replaced."

"The land's still there. You can rebuild and start over."

"But do I want to? Look how quickly it can all be taken away. In the blink of an eye."

Gently, Zach drew her back against his chest. "You'll feel differently later."

"Maybe." Yet, what else would she do with her life? She was thirty-one years old, and though she had her accounting degree, the only thing she'd done since college—the only thing she'd *wanted* since then, other than the boy she'd loved and the parents Fate had taken from her—was to run her shop.

"Come on," he said, turning her around to face him. "I'm parked beside your van. Let's drive over to that convenience store on the other end of town and get a cup of coffee or a cold drink. You need to get away from here for a while."

She shook her head. "I can't go anywhere. My clothes reek from the fire."

"So what?" he said, trying to coax a grin from her. "I'm wearing yesterday's socks. There's nothing you can do about any of this right now. We'll just grab something to drink, and when we come back, we'll check in with the fire chief to see if there's any more news."

Kristin pushed out of his arms, giving in to frustration instead of tears. "Then what, since you seem to have all the answers? What will we do then?"

His tone remained unchanged. "Then we'll sit in my truck for as long as you need to be here. All night, if necessary. In the morning, if you need help contacting your insurance company or anyone else, or if you need to board up the windows, I'm your guy."

No, he wasn't. He hadn't been her guy for a very long time. But tonight…tonight there was no one else to cling to. "Okay," she said through a sigh. "I'd love a cup of coffee."

"Good," he replied with a smile. Draping an arm over her shoulders, he walked her up the grassy hill toward Eli's lot. "I have a cell phone if you want to call anyone. It's three hours earlier in Arizona if you'd like to talk to your sister. Or," he added half-heartedly, "I could call her for you."

"Thanks, but no." The second Rachel heard his voice, not only would she be certain Zach started the fire, she'd be calling the local psychiatric ward to have Kristin committed for even speaking to him again. For a psychologist who was supposed to have an open mind, Rachel's was shut, locked and manacled where Zach was concerned. She'd held Kristin while she cried on too many occasions to be forgiving of the man responsible for the tears.

"I'll phone her in the morning," she said as they reached his truck. "Maybe I'll have more news by then."

Only a dozen firefighters and three trucks remained when they returned an hour later and pulled into the bookstore's lot. They'd ended up sitting outside the convenience store in Zach's truck to drink their coffees, the coward in Kristin in no hurry to return once she'd left.

Now, most of the onlookers and linemen from the electric company had gone, too. While the last tendrils of ash and smoke dissipated into the air, firemen hung close to the trucks, drinking from foam cups and speaking in subdued tones.

Zach spoke soberly. "Want to stay here for a minute while I speak to the firemen? Or would you rather do it?"

"No, you go ahead. I'm feeling a little too beaten to ask again if anything survived."

His gentle look said he understood. "I won't be long."

And he wasn't. When he returned a few minutes later, his eyes were soft and sympathetic. "It's pretty much finished," he said. "They're just hanging around to make sure there are no flare-ups. Someone said it looks like the roof might stay up. That'll make it easier for the fire marshal to determine the cause. Less rubble to sift through."

Kristin swallowed. Everything she'd worked for, everything she'd built and treasured was gone. Her pretty shop had replaced so many things over the years. It had replaced family. It had replaced love and marriage and children. It had replaced Zach.

Now what?

Tears she'd kept at bay for the past several hours slid down her cheeks.

Zach pushed the black leather bench seat as far back from the steering wheel as it would go and gathered her close. She came to him without reservation and clung tightly.

"It'll be okay," he murmured. "It might not seem that way now, but you're a strong woman, and you'll find a way to make it okay."

"Strong?" she sobbed. "Just look at me! I'm not strong."

"Yes, you are. Look what you've done so far—not

the least of which is putting yourself through college and building a thriving business out of a trinket shop. You're going to be fine.''

Would she? She had her doubts. Even in the cab of the truck with the windows rolled up, she could smell the fire and it *hurt*. It overshadowed the masculine smell of leather, overshadowed the faint scent of soap that still clung to Zach's skin. She drove her nose into his shirt, trying to replace the smell of loss with the smell of life.

''Hey,'' he murmured, and tipped her face up to his.

''What?''

''Just this.'' His kiss was gentle and compassionate and tender, a brief brushing of lips, a brief meeting of gray eyes full of caring and understanding.

''Thank you for being with me,'' she whispered when they'd parted. ''When I was standing with Eli and the others I felt like I was coming apart at the seams. But I couldn't let them see that.'' She tried to smile. ''Thanks for letting me come apart at the seams.''

Zach untangled a few long strands of her bangs from her lashes. ''I owe you this much. There was a time when you needed me and I wasn't there for you.''

It wasn't an admission of guilt, only an admission that he had regrets and wanted to repay a debt. But tonight, unlike his apology the day of her mother's funeral, she believed what he said.

Time sighed and stretched out like a weary dog that was too tired to fight anymore. Kristin put that old hurt behind her for now, letting the hollow canyon in her chest begin to shrink a little.

She didn't know who eased into the kiss first, Zach or herself. But it was as welcome as a warm spring rain, comforting her heart, filling those empty spots burned out by the fire, and waking her to the magic of emotional connection. She deepened the kiss, taking more of his strength and caring and using them to restore herself.

She never noticed the subtle difference in the kiss, never noticed that it had somehow shifted from compassion to wanting until it was too late to stop it.

By then she didn't want to.

Chapter 6

The kiss was intoxicating...tantalizing, a whirlpool of sensation dragging her down into an undertow of forgotten passion.

Kristin drew his scent deep into her lungs, drove her hands through his thick black hair, opened to him as he ground his hot, hard mouth over hers and plunged his tongue inside.

The trembling low in her abdomen spread like wildfire as Zach slid his hand under her sweatshirt. His breathing was labored, his kiss bottomless as his fingertips slid languidly over her exposed skin, stealing her breath and easing upward. Then he was smoothing his warm hand over lace-edged cotton, and murmuring that it had been so long. When callused fingers slid inside to cup her softness and he claimed her mouth again, Kristin was lost.

She worked her eager hands up under his shirt, her

nerves on fire as she encountered chest hair and hard muscle.

Zach broke from the kiss to bury his face in her neck, reached behind her to unhook her bra.

Hurry, hurry, Kristin's mind repeated as he fumbled with the catch. She wanted him, wanted all of him.

But Zach's continued tugs when hooks and eyes wouldn't budge broke through her haze.

Kristin stopped his hands as alarm bells went off in her head, and she forced herself to breathe, to think.

She couldn't do this. Not here. *Not anywhere.* She'd lost her shop. Was she losing her mind as well? They weren't lovers anymore, they were…

What? Was there a term for old lovers who couldn't keep their hands to themselves?

Sighing raggedly, Zach rolled away to settle back against the black leather upholstery and stare through the windshield. Kristin inched closer to her door.

Faint, outside sounds found their way inside the truck through Zach's partially-open window as their breathing struggled for a sensible rhythm. An occasional car motor as the fire police rerouted light traffic…the quiet conversation of volunteers who'd brought food and beverages to the firefighters. Even the low gurgle of water still running down the street and into storm drains.

"Should I say I'm sorry?" he murmured after a while.

Kristin swallowed, training her attention on the fire trucks below because it was too painful to look at her shop, and too uncomfortable to look at Zach. "Are you?"

"No. I enjoyed it. I think you did, too."

"Old habits die hard," she admitted, neither agreeing nor disagreeing. She found the courage to meet his eyes. "Thank you for holding me. I needed that just then. But the other…well, that was…"

"Just something that happened? Too much emotion in one night? Another lapse in judgment?"

"It was probably all of those things." But it was more, too. Not lingering feelings of love, but something. A flush of arousal moved through her as she relived the heat of his kisses, the raw masculine taste and touch of him. But despite the pleasure she'd felt, they'd made another mistake, and mistakes carried consequences. She didn't even want to think what they might be.

"Are you all right?" she asked.

"I'm getting there."

She hoped so. One of them should be, and it certainly wasn't her. "I think I'd like to rest my eyes for a while if you don't mind," she said hesitantly, then realized with regret that he might prefer that she do it elsewhere. Passion eased more quickly if the participants didn't have to deal with one another's closeness.

She motioned to her white van, only a few yards away. "Maybe I should rest over there. Then you could go back to the farmhouse and get some sleep."

"If you'll be more comfortable resting in your van, go ahead. But I'm not going anywhere. Do you want to be alone?"

Kristin shook her head. "No," she admitted. "I just want being here with you to be less…stressful." Less exciting. Less needy. Less dangerous.

"Okay." Zach reached behind him to grab a thick blanket from the back seat, and Kristin stilled as he slid close. She was nearly pressed against the door, but there was room for him to tuck the blanket behind her back. The heat of his body, his very nearness, brought back those feelings of attraction again, and she almost reconsidered going to her van.

"Sleep if you want. If the fire chief or any of his men need to talk to you, they know where we're parked." He tapped the split backs on the truck's bench seat. "These recline if you want to be more comfortable."

Recline? That's all they needed. "No, I don't need to sleep," she answered quickly. "I just need to close my eyes for a few minutes." *And distance myself from you.*

But she did sleep. In a matter of minutes, her head was lolling against the window and she was completely out.

Zach stared at her delicate profile in the dusky light, his mind wandering down paths and trails he had no business visiting. She was so beautiful, and so wounded, and there was nothing he could do to make any of it right for her. She didn't deserve this, not after everything she'd already been through.

What would have happened if she'd told him the truth about her mother's condition all those years ago? he wondered. Would they be together now? Married? Maybe with a couple of kids?

Without conscious direction, his gaze fell to her flat stomach and he imagined her carrying his child. Then, in the way that one thought triggers another and another, he envisioned her chasing a tiny, giggling replica of herself along the shell-studded sand below his Nags Head beach house. He could hear frothy breakers crashing on the evening shore…hear the mocking cries of the gulls winging overhead. He smiled, seeing Kris overtake the little girl. Then, laughing, she scooped the wriggling toddler up and lifted her high against a painted sky.

Zach broke free of the image and scowled. Well, wasn't that dramatic? Why, he should call Hollywood. Hey, Spielberg, Zach Davis has a can't-miss screenplay for you.

Shaking his head, he rolled down the window a little, letting in some cool air and a whiff of stale smoke. Why was he wondering about things he didn't want—didn't have time for? His life was phoning for estimates, bidding on jobs, butting heads with unions, overseeing his crews and pouring over his books. Most days, he even ended up working beside his men. He barely had time for a casual date and some no-strings sex, let alone anything long-term. The absolute last thing he needed was the responsibility of a wife and family.

Not that he hadn't thought about it a night or two when sleep wouldn't come...

But not now. Not until his business was firmly established and he had something to offer his kids. He'd never hand them the legacy of poverty and shame his father had left him.

Zach stretched a hand back to flip up the back seat, then reached past Kristin to release the lever beside her door. Gently, he eased her seat back as far at it would go and draped the blanket over her lap. A moment later, his seat was tilted back, too.

Stacking his hands behind his head, he looked up at the sky, stars once hidden by smoke finally visible through the windshield. The possibility of having a family gathered shape in his mind. He'd love to have a little girl one day—a couple of boys, too. Boys who could carry on the business when he was too old to swing a hammer and finally bring some honor to the family name.

Although, he thought wryly, he didn't see how he could father any child—boy or girl—if he couldn't even unhook a damn bra.

A sharp crack shattered their sleep. Zach's eyes flew open to sunlight streaming through his windshield at the same time Kris's did. They lay there, nearly flat on their backs beneath the blanket, nose to nose and tangled in each other's arms. Unless he was still dreaming, his left hand under the blanket was cupping Kristin's nicely rounded bottom.

Vaulting upright, she skittered away like a startled fiddler crab, her flustered expression telling him she wasn't pleased with the way they'd ended up.

The tall, blond man peering down through Kristin's window—and probably the source of that jarring noise—didn't look happy, either.

Hiding a smile, Zach decided that his day was made.

"Chad!" Kristin said in a relieved rush. Tossing the blanket on the floor, she left the truck, finger-combing her tousled hair.

Zach's stomach clenched as Hollister set a take-out bag on the hood of Zach's truck and took her in his arms. Her voice rose as she blurted out everything she knew about the fire, every upsetting scrap of information she had.

"I know," Hollister crooned, rocking her close. "I saw the police report Larry put on my desk. Oh, honey, I'm so sorry."

Zach yanked the low lever beside him, catapulted his seat straight up, and went outside.

"I'm so sorry I wasn't here," Hollister murmured into her hair. "What can I do to make this easier for you?"

Kristin eased away to look down on the charred remains of her shop, her shoulders slumping dejectedly. "Nothing. There's nothing anyone can do, but knowing you want to helps. Thank you."

Zach looked at the shop, too. Night and billowing smoke had hidden the horrific damage the fire had inflicted. Now, in the light of day, there was no denying that she'd lost everything. Her once pretty shop lay shapeless and ruined. Even part of the roof had come down in the night. The firefighters and fire police who'd stayed stood talking somberly, like mourners at a wake.

Kristin blinked to clear the glaze from her eyes. "Thank heaven someone had the presence of mind to move the wooden gliders and swings I sell for the Stoltzfus family away from the building. They made it through, at least."

She sighed, then, and turned toward the yellow tape roping off the street. "Excuse me for a minute. Maybe there's news—something they learned during the night."

Chad pulled her back. "Kristin, don't go down there. It'll just make you feel worse. I've already spoken to them, and there's nothing new to report."

Defiance flashed in her eyes as she pulled away. "But *I* haven't spoken to them yet, and it was my shop. I'll be right back."

Obviously startled, Chad released her, watched her leave, then turned to finally acknowledge Zach's presence. "Morning, Davis," he said.

"Morning," Zach replied curtly.

Hollister went to the take-out bag on the truck's hood, retrieved a large foam cup of coffee for himself, then stunned Zach by handing him a cup. "Here. Figured you'd need an eye-opener this morning, too."

Zach wasn't often struck speechless, but Hollister's unexpected consideration did it for him. He didn't stay speechless long. "Thanks. But why?"

Chad's reply was grudgingly polite. "It's the least I could do after you stood in for me last night. I was sick when I got back and heard about the fire."

Every nerve in Zach's body jerked at being labeled Hollister's "stand in," and it took every ounce of his self-control to keep him from telling Chad just how *well* he'd stood in for him. The only thing that kept his lips sealed was the knowledge that mouthing off would put Kris in an awkward spot. She was dealing with enough right now.

Besides, in his own asinine way, Chad was being decent, despite the little scene he'd walked up on this morning. Hollister's bringing three cups of coffee made it clear that he'd either seen them in the truck earlier, or had learned from his deputy that Kristin had spent the night in Zach's truck.

They drank for a while, both of their gazes locked on Kris as she spoke with the firefighters. Then Chad took another sip and said, out of the blue, "You left, I stayed. She needed someone to hold on to, and I was there."

"Are you looking for my thanks, or are you trying to make a point?"

"Making a point." The sun glinted off Hollister's mirrored sunglasses as his gaze remained fixed on Kristin. "I love her. She'll be my wife one day, you know."

Not if she has a brain in her head. "To be honest, Chad, I doubt that. Mrs. Chase died over nine years ago. What's taken you so long to put a ring on her finger?"

Hollister finished his coffee and stuck the empty cup into the bag. "She needed time after her mother died to find out who she was. From high school graduation on, she was basically a nurse. Her sister helped, but Rachel was finishing college, so most of Mrs. Chase's care came from Kristin. Afterward, she went to school, came back and started the shop." He paused. "She needed to gain some confidence—build a life of her own before she was ready to share it with someone else."

He removed his glasses and tucked them in his breast pocket. "I wanted her," he went on. "I've always wanted her. But a man has to do what's right. It would've been wrong to rush her."

Zach couldn't disagree.

Chad slipped his hands into the pockets of his uniform trousers, his gaze back on Kristin. "But now, it's time we started making plans for our future. When are you going back home?"

Zach's first inclination was to tell him it was none of his business. But what was the point? "Two weeks, give or take a day."

Hollister nodded complacently, then turned to Zach. "Let us know where to reach you. We'll see that you get an invitation to the wedding."

Zach bristled, his hands aching to curl into fists. The son of a bitch really enjoyed putting it to him—even when there was no reason to consider him a rival anymore.

Kristin's approach broke the clash of their gazes,

her sneakers moving briskly and purposefully up the grassy hill to the lot. She shoved the sleeves of her gray sweatshirt back, her dark eyes flashing, her color high.

"Why didn't you tell me?" she demanded, storming up to Hollister.

Though Zach was completely in the dark, Chad's crestfallen expression told Zach he knew exactly what Kris was referring to.

"I planned to," he replied in a voice that tried to calm her. "I just wanted to wait until we were alone. It's not even official yet. It's merely supposition until we get the marshal's ruling."

"I still had a right to know."

Hollister sighed. "I'm sorry. I was just trying to spare you for a little while."

She stared at him for a time, seconds turning into moments, the moments rife with tension. Then slowly, she let go of her anger and nodded toward the street. "They need you down there. Something about rerouting traffic for a while longer."

"Okay, just don't be mad, all right? I was thinking of you."

Kristin nodded, then Hollister hugged her briefly, murmured something Zach couldn't hear, and left.

Zach dumped the rest of Chad's gift-coffee into the gravel, took the bag from the hood of his truck and wandered over to Kristin.

He handed her her cup, then jammed his empty one inside the bag and crunched the whole works in his hands. "What's up?"

"They suspect arson."

"Arson?"

Kristin nodded, a stray breeze tossing her bangs.

"Al Miller—the husband of one of my regular customers—said he thinks it was an accelerant fire. He
and some of the others smelled kerosene when they
arrived. Apparently, gasoline fumes disappear quickly,
but kerosene lingers."

Tears shone in her eyes again. "If that's true, it
means that someone deliberately destroyed my shop.
Who would do that?" she demanded on a plea. "I
don't have enemies."

Zach drew her close again, wondering if it felt this
good to hold her because he wanted to piss off Hollister, or because it was Kristin in his arms. She felt
so small, so fragile. "Much as I hate to agree with
anything Chad says, he's right. It's just a guess right
now. Wait until the fire marshal checks things out before you jump to conclusions."

Backing away, she pulled her keys from the pocket
of her jeans. "That's another thing. The fire marshal
won't be able to get to it for at least four days, maybe
a week. He's investigating another fire right now."

Zach fell into step beside her as she walked around
the front of his truck, then to the driver's side of her
late model, white-and-blue custom van. Forget Me Not
Antiques was painted on the side in silver-edged blue,
all loopy script within a ring of tiny pink and blue
flowers. He experienced a twinge looking at it.

"What now?" he asked.

"Home to take a shower, then I'll start calling people. The insurance company first. Then Rachel, then
the utility companies, then…" She drew a deep breath
and let it out wearily. "I don't know who else. It'll
come to me."

"Want some help?"

Kristin shook her head, the confidence and direction

he'd seen in her yesterday slowly returning. "Thanks, but no. I need to pull myself together and stop leaning on other people. That's not my way."

"All right," he said, his pride in her increasing as he took his wallet from his back pocket. He withdrew a business card, then glanced at the back of it before he extended it to her. "If you change your mind, the chicken-scratching on the back is my cell phone number. I'll be at the farmhouse."

Hesitantly, Kristin took the card, then looked up at him. "Chad said he'd see if one of his deputies could work for him today, so he'll be around...."

Masking a stab of jealousy, Zach forced a careless shrug. "Oh. That's fine."

"Thanks for putting me up for the night, though," she said with a tired smile. "I really didn't want to be alone."

"No problem," he said, closing her door when she got inside. "Take care of yourself."

"You, too."

But it was a problem, he thought a few hours later—*she* was a problem. Because for the rest of the morning and most of the afternoon, he couldn't do a damn thing right to save his soul. He'd ruined two planks, burned the hamburgers he'd put on the grill for lunch and just generally screwed up everything he touched. He kept seeing her in his mind, alternately strong and focused, then uncertain and sad.

Of course, the ever-helpful *Chad* would be there for her, Zach remembered, going back inside the house to grab his keys and change to a fresh shirt.

By two o'clock, he was at the building supply house outside of town, buying new porch lights and more lumber to replace the boards he'd cut too short. Then he went through Burger Bear's drive-thru for a more palatable lunch. He was on his way back when he passed a patrol car with its lights flashing and saw Hollister ticketing an out-of-state driver.

A rush of adrenaline hit him. *Chad hadn't found anyone to work for him. Kris was alone.* Zach pushed his boot down a little harder on the accelerator and headed back to the Burger Bear to use their phone book.

Kris was just getting out of her van when Zach pulled into the driveway behind her. She was carrying something wrapped in aluminum foil.

"Late lunch or an early dinner?" he asked casually, getting out and nodding at the package.

"Neither," she said with a rueful smile. "Cinnamon rolls, piping hot from the oven. I just got back from Mrs. Zimm's home. The Amish don't have telephones, so I had to drive out to tell her I wouldn't be able to sell her baked goods anymore. At least not for a while. She insisted that I take these."

"She sounds like a nice woman."

"She really is," Kristin replied, then assessed him curiously. "What are you doing here?"

Smiling, Zach took in her pretty face and sun-struck hair, the navy-and-white-striped top she wore with crisp white slacks and deck shoes. She looked beautiful and fresh and strong, despite the pain and disappointment she was feeling underneath. No doubt about it, Kristin Chase was a trouper. A delicate gold sailboat hung from a chain around her neck.

"What am I doing here?" he repeated, his smile increasing. "I guess I must have smelled warm cinnamon rolls."

Kristin stared for a second, then shook her head and allowed a smile to edge her lips. He was glad she didn't press him for a better explanation because he didn't have one.

"Come on." She nodded toward the flower-lined walk leading to the beige-and-white town house's front porch. "I'll make coffee. We'll have a picnic."

When they were settled on the small, tree-shaded patio off her living room, Kristin repeated the question. This time he had to give her an honest answer.

"I was worried about you," Zach answered. "You weren't in the best of shape when we said goodbye this morning. Then I saw Chad ticketing some guy along the road and knew you were probably alone. I didn't want you to be, so I looked up your address in the phone book."

"I was fine."

"But I didn't know that."

Her soft smile thanked him.

Zach looked around as she moved the pot of leafy pink roses to the flagstone floor to make room for the cinnamon rolls, then filled their cups from a white carafe. She had a decorator's touch. Their white china plates sat atop woven hunter green place mats on the glass table, and matching hunter-green cushions covered the seats of her white wrought-iron chairs. More roses climbed a trellis beside the sparkling patio doors, and big clay pots spilled over with the same kind of pink, white and lavender flowers that lined her walk. When a gray squirrel chattered his irritation at songbirds chirping in a nearby maple tree, Zach decided that this was no picnic. It was a Disney movie.

Kristin slid her pink-flowered napkin from a white ring and placed it on her lap. Feeling awkward, Zach did the same, glad his crew couldn't see him. He was out of his element, but there was no point in looking like a barbarian.

He helped himself to a cinnamon roll. "I like your place."

"Thanks. I like it, too. I almost kept my mom's house, but after I got out of school, I decided there were too many unhappy memories there. I wanted to start fresh."

"That's understandable." He'd wanted to start a new life from the time he was eight and recognized his old life for what it was.

His gaze moved over her classic features again, drinking in her wide brown eyes...lingering on soft lips that, not so long ago, had returned his fevered kisses with equal passion and left him quaking like a school kid. It was no surprise when a purely male response stirred beneath his napkin.

"It looks like I worried for nothing. You look better, more accepting." He smiled. "And pretty."

Cheeks coloring, Kristin sipped from her cup, then returned it to her saucer. "I have to accept. I don't have any choice. Still, when I think of everything that burned, it hurts. As I told you last night, I'm well covered, but heaven knows how long it will take my insurance company to settle my claim. Especially if they suspect arson."

Zach nodded grimly as he chewed a bite of his roll. The insurance company would have to rule out any involvement on Kristin's part before they paid up— that was a given. But depending upon the company, if the fire was deliberately set and no arrest was made, it could be months until she saw a dime.

''Did you call your sister?'' he asked. Hopefully, Rachel had had some comforting things to say.

''Not yet. She was with a client, so I told Addie— her receptionist—that I'd call back later.''

The phone rang just then, startling them both. But it was Zach's cell phone that needed answering, not hers. Grinning, he took the small unit from the pocket of his chambray shirt. ''Maybe that's Rachel now.''

''Now that would be a first,'' Kristin said, laughing. The only reason Rachel would call Zach was to give him another piece of her mind.

But less than a minute into the conversation, Kristin watched Zach's features cloud, and she excused herself to refill their carafe and give him some privacy.

She needed some privacy, too. The jitters she'd been feeling since he arrived were wreaking havoc— a fact that was fairly evident when she spilled coffee all over her countertop as she transferred it from her coffeemaker to the carafe.

Grabbing a sponge from the sink, she mopped up the puddle, thinking how strange life was. Three days ago, she wouldn't have given Zach Davis the time of day if she'd had an armful of wristwatches. Now they were sitting across a table like old friends. She couldn't begin to fathom how that had come about. One moment they were slinging insults at each other, the next...the next, he was kissing her senseless and she was melting in his arms.

Zach walked inside as she was leaving the kitchen, his expression troubled. Kristin paused in the doorway. He was so big, so darkly masculine that he seemed to leech the color from her peach-and-mint décor until the only thing she saw was him.

''What's wrong?'' she asked nervously.

"That was my foreman. I'm sorry, but I have to head back to Nags Head. A problem's come up that needs my attention."

Kristin stilled. She would've thought she'd feel relief, not this sinking disappointment. "I'm sorry to hear that. I hope it's nothing too serious."

"Me, too," he replied grimly.

Moistening her lips, she shrugged. "Well...thanks for stopping by."

But Zach didn't move. He stood there for a long moment, his gray gaze full of turmoil and seemingly torn by indecision.

She nearly dropped the carafe on the floor when he finally spoke.

"Come with me," he said quietly.

"What?"

"Come with me," he repeated, more strength and certainty in his voice now. "I've already called the airport. There's a flight leaving in two hours. That should give you plenty of time to pack."

Chapter 7

"I—I can't do that."

"Why not?" Zach strolled a little closer to her. "It would be good for you—the sun, the sand, the ocean. They could be just what you need right now. Have you ever been to the Outer Banks?"

"No, but—"

"Then you owe this to yourself. There'll never be a better time. Remember when we thought we'd be living there? We talked about swimming and looking for shells...."

Yes, they had. They'd also talked about making love on the beach every night. Gretchen had put a stop to that. "That was a long time ago."

"I realize that. But those things are still there. You could swim, collect shells, read while you sunbathe...but mostly, you could regroup. You could think about where you want to go from here without any distractions."

Kristin shook her head, bewildered that he could suggest such a thing. "Zach, I have responsibilities here. I can't just pack up and leave."

"What responsibilities?"

"Have you forgotten that I have a major mess to clean up?"

"Have you forgotten that you can't touch anything until the fire marshal has investigated—which, you just told me won't be for the better part of a week? We'll be back by then. What's the real reason you won't go? Chad?"

Sighing, Kristin went to her sofa, set the carafe beside the leafy green centerpiece on the coffee table, and sank to the cushions. It was time for honesty.

"No. It's not because of Chad. Chad and I are friends who see a movie or have dinner occasionally. That's all. I know he wants more, but I don't see that happening right now."

The look on Zach's face wasn't what she expected. Considering his and Chad's antagonistic past, she'd expected smug approval, maybe a gleam of satisfaction. But the thoughts moving through Zach's eyes weren't even close to that. In fact, he seemed to be taken aback, faintly troubled by her admission.

It was several moments before he walked to the sofa and sat down beside her, looking out of place amid her feminine furnishings. Her peach-and-mint florals, brass accents and glass tables clashed badly with strong, tanned man and blue denim. A sudden breeze through the patio doors lifted the white sheers beneath her drapes...tossed the dark hair falling over Zach's forehead.

"All right, if it's not Chad, then what's stopping you?"

Kristin stared in disbelief. "You can't guess?" Couldn't he feel the coiled tension, the persistent awareness between them, even now?

He didn't say anything for a few seconds, then he nodded soberly, those gray eyes penetrating hers until she felt so unstrung, she had to get up. Walking out to the patio, she started clearing the table.

"It wouldn't be a problem," Zach said, following her.

"Really?" Kristin retrieved a serving tray from the seat of an unused chair, then started stacking their plates and silverware. "Where do you see me staying?"

"At my beach house, where I spend very little time, and where we'd each have our own bedrooms. If that makes you uneasy, I can sleep at the trailer."

Kristin kept working, avoiding his gaze, disturbed that they were even addressing the issue of chemistry. To address it meant admitting that the attraction still existed, and that made her feel vulnerable. "Sleep at a construction trailer instead of your own home?"

"During the summer months, I work twelve- to sixteen-hour days, every day. It wouldn't be the first time I bunked there."

Zach took the plates from her hands, added them to the tray and forced her to look at him. "I didn't want to bring this up, but *if* the fire was deliberately set, I'd worry about you. I know you have friends, and I know Chad would look out for you. But he has to work. And as far as family goes, you have no one but Rachel, and she's in Arizona. You're too alone here, Kris."

The implication struck her like a thunderclap, along with the realization of just how alone in this world she really was. She had cousins and aunts and uncles, but they all lived several states away. Her heart began to pound, fear stepping in for the first time. "You think—"

"No, I don't think anyone wants to hurt you personally. If that were the case, I doubt the fire would've been at the shop."

No, it probably would have been here, at her home. Gooseflesh cropped up on her arms.

"Still, setting a fire does send a message that someone's pretty ticked off. *If* it was an arson. Come with me. I should be able to take care of my business in two days—three at the most. You have a lot of work ahead of you. You need to step back and take a few deep breaths before you begin."

Kristin studied the caring and compassion in his eyes, wondering where those tender emotions had been the night he'd ruined their dreams. Had they been buried beneath doubts and insecurity as he'd claimed? Because there was no sign of that now.

Not that it mattered. What mattered now was the problem at hand, and he was right about that. Searching through the ashes of her shop to see if anything had survived would cut to the core. Watching men clear away the rubble until nothing remained but an empty lot would hurt even more. Maybe she did need to ready herself for what was to come. Maybe...

"All right," she agreed quietly.

"All right what?"

"I'll go. Thank you."

Releasing a relieved blast of air, Zach pulled her close, and without thinking, Kristin hugged him back, grateful for his warmth and his strength.

He smiled as he released her. "I'll see myself out

and be back to pick you up in an hour. Don't forget to pack a swimsuit and something to read.''

"I won't."

A minute later, Kristin waved a tentative goodbye to him from the patio, her pulse racing again. Was she in danger? Had she unknowingly made an enemy who wanted to ruin her? Or was the real danger in going off with a man she was beginning to care about again?

Piling the remaining dishes on the tray, she took them to the sink, then went to her room to pack. She'd nearly finished stuffing her carry-on when she spied Anna Mae's diaries on top of her bureau and added them, too. If she hadn't been so rattled last night and scooped them up with her purse and paperwork, they'd be gone now, along with everything else.

Before she'd driven out to the Zimm's, she'd phoned Mildred Arnett to ask if she wanted the journals. But the strange woman had balked at the very idea, insisting that the words of the dead weren't for the living to read. She'd even worried that Anna Mae's spirit might have started the fire in Kristin's shop— that maybe none of her cousin's belongings should have been taken from the "death house." Maybe *she*—Mildred—was even courting danger by having some of Anna Mae's things in her home.

Still dumbfounded by Mildred's quick goodbye to phone her psychic, Kristin carried her bag to the living room, then started the dishes.

The lunacy of what she was about to do hit her full force as she stared at the plates she and Zach had used.

Her life was a soap opera. She'd been hurt in a break-in, her shop had burned—possibly at the hands of an arsonist, she had dealings with a woman who consulted a psychic and now she was flying off to stay at an ex-lover's beach house. All she needed was a case of amnesia and an evil twin for a starring role in a daytime drama.

Sighing, Kristin recalled the new message she'd left on Rachel's answering machine. Her sister was going to hit the roof.

The flight to the Outer Banks was smooth and uneventful, and true to Zach's foreman's word, Zach's dark blue, canvas-topped Jeep was waiting in the short-term parking lot when they arrived. Now as they climbed the weathered gray steps to the wraparound deck of his equally weathered house on stilts, Kristin couldn't keep a smile from her lips. Striding to the railing, she inhaled deeply while the salt breeze tossed her hair. She took in everything at once—the sea, the sand, the blue sky. Even the faint, but not unpleasant smell of shellfish.

There was a freedom here she'd never felt before, an energy, yet peace, she'd never experienced. Probably because she was so far away from her troubles. Some distance out, white caps rose and swelled, then raced to shore and broke on the beach in a frothy spray. Overhead, noisy gulls wheeled and banked, venting their displeasure as a fireball sun slowly descended to the water.

"It's paradise," she murmured, smiling back at him. "And it's yours?"

Zach chuckled as he unlocked the door and carried their bags inside the house. "Well, I generally share the sand and water, but the house is mine as long as I pay the rent." He lifted his voice to be heard outside. "You should hang out on the deck for a while and enjoy the sunset. They're beautiful, but they happen in the blink of an eye. If you get busy inside, you'll miss it.''

Kristin turned toward the bank of windows fronting the deck as Zach cranked them open and spoke through the screens. ''I have to run out and pick up some groceries. I hadn't planned on coming back for another two weeks, so there's not much in my refrigerator.''

Her spirits sank a little. ''Aren't you staying for the sunset?''

He came back out, his keys in one hand, a can of insect repellent in the other. ''Not tonight. It's getting late, and I still have a dozen things to take care of before I close my eyes.''

''Oh. Okay.'' She sent him a questioning look when he handed her the bug spray.

''Even paradise has its drawbacks. I'm pretty sure they sprayed for mosquitoes while I was gone, but keep that handy just in case. Now—is takeout okay for dinner?''

''Sure. Or I could fix something.''

''Uh-uh. You're here for rest and relaxation. Pizza? Chinese? Burgers? What's your pleasure? I'd rather save a seafood dinner for a night when we'll have more time to enjoy it.''

He was in a hurry. In fact, he looked ready to leap off the deck to the sand-speckled blacktop below. It was a side of him she'd never seen, almost as though returning home had triggered some kind of driven behavior.

''Pizza with everything but anchovies?'' she suggested, recalling that he liked it that way, too.

''Sounds good. I'll be back in a half hour—forty-five minutes, tops. Feel free to take the tour. I put your

things in the room across the hall from the bathroom.''
Then he was down the steps and, seconds later, driving
away.

Kristin blinked, feeling a bit like a hit-and-run vic-
tim.

Dragging a deck chair close to the bleached railing,
she curled into it and watched the sun burn its way to
the ocean, laying a shimmering trail of red and gold
over the water. It truly was beautiful. Just the same,
she felt less warmed by the spectacle than she'd expected to be, because Zach wasn't there to share it
with her. And that bothered her.

Compared to the exterior, the interior of the house
was a cozy surprise. Though it was nothing like her
décor at home, a comfortable couch and loveseat in
nubby beige sat in an L-shaped arrangement, piled
with throw pillows in turquoise, coral and ivory, and
flanked by glass-topped wooden parson's tables and
no-nonsense lamps. A deck of playing cards sat on the
matching coffee table in front of the sofa, and conch
shells in assorted sizes adorned the entertainment center that held his TV, stereo and VCR. Framed sea-
scapes hung on the white wood-paneled walls.

Slipping off her sneakers, Kristin crossed the pale
Berber carpet to the open kitchen where oak cupboards, white appliances and black-and-gray mottled
countertops nearly gleamed. Behind a bar with stools,
a round oak table with four chairs looked out through
another bank of windows to the deck. She smiled, de-
ciding that he was a pretty fair housekeeper.

She'd settled into the guest room, and was just setting the table when Zach came inside juggling a large
pizza box and two bags full of groceries. Instantly, the

anxiety she'd managed to ignore while she acclimated herself to her surroundings was back.

"I see you found the dishes."

"You gave me permission to snoop," she said, shrugging. "I snooped."

"Good." He put the pizza and bags in the middle of the table. "Is your room okay? I rent this place furnished for the most part, so the decorating choices aren't my own." He grinned. "Not that I'd be able to come up with anything better."

"My room's fine. Thanks."

"You're welcome. Did you look around downstairs?" When she shook her head, he said, "There's a washer and dryer down there, and just outside the garage, there's another deck and an outdoor shower. Use whatever you want. *Mi casa es su casa.*"

At least for the next few days, she thought as a funny feeling collected in her stomach. She finished placing silverware on their napkins, then with a brief glance at him, she nodded at the bags on the table. "Any chance you bought milk?"

"Of course. We always drink milk with pizza."

Kristin went still. Zach did, too, as the familiarity of that phrase hung in the air. Then he pulled the gallon jug out of the bag, said, "I'll fill our glasses," and the moment was over.

Conversation flowed easily during dinner, primarily because they discussed Zach's reason for rushing home—a disgruntled client who'd threatened to break her contract if Zach didn't personally oversee the building of her new beach house.

"But if she's already signed the contract, she doesn't really have a leg to stand on, does she?"

"Technically, no. But I don't like strong-arming clients."

"So what are you going to do?" Kristin asked, knowing he'd only allotted three days to smooth over the matter.

"Talk to her, reassure her…give her my word that the second I finish Etta's renovations, I'll be on the job. She's extremely well-to-do and has influential friends. I want her recommending Davis Construction to all of them." He drank from his glass, then grinned wryly. "I guess she's entitled to gripe a little. Her deal was with me. It's understandable that she'd want me at the site now and then."

Zach's gaze fell to the gold necklace lying against the white knit top Kristin had worn on their flight. "By the way, I like your sailboat."

"Thanks," she said with a faint smile. "It was a gift from my mom. After her diagnosis, she gave one to me and one to Rachel. She said whenever we felt low, to just lift it to our lips and blow a little more air into our sails, and we'd be okay."

"Been doing that a lot lately, huh?"

He'd never know how much, or that often, he was the cause. "Yep."

When dinner was through and they'd straightened up the kitchen, Kristin sat on the couch flicking through channels on the TV, her awkwardness returning. Being under the same roof with him was doable when they were talking about things that had no bearing on their relationship—rather, former relationship—or if she had busy work to do. But now…

Now, she just wanted to get ready for bed. But with Zach on the phone with his foreman in the office next to the bathroom, the idea of undressing and showering put her on edge. Adding to her discomfort, she was having second thoughts about his driving to a construction trailer to sleep when it was nearly eleven o'clock. How could she ask him to do that when he'd been so kind and generous—first at the fire, and now here?

She straightened abruptly on the couch as the office door shut, and Zach carried a duffel bag into the living room.

"Okay, I'm out of here," he said offhandedly. "You still have my business card with all the phone numbers, right?"

"Yes, it's in my purse." That's where she'd found his home phone number to leave on Rachel's answering machine. In her rush to pack, she'd forgotten to call her sister back at the office. Or maybe she'd put it out of her mind because she knew Rachel wouldn't react well to this trip.

"Okay, then. Call if you need anything. And lock up after me. The people in the other houses are mostly vacationing families, so there's probably nothing to worry about, but lock up and close the blinds in your room anyway. I've already taken care of the rest of them."

That did it. Kristin came to her feet. She couldn't stay here surrounded by strangers, not after everything she'd been through in the past few days. "Wait," she called as he reached the door.

He turned. "Did I forget something?"

"No, I...I don't want you to go."

Deep furrows lined his brow and he hesitated for a long moment. "Are you sure?"

She nodded. "There's no good reason for you to leave. This is your home."

Slowly, he slid the door's deadbolt in place, then turned back to her. "Okay. Then I think I'll get some shut-eye. I'll be out of here tomorrow before you wake up, but I'll phone sometime in the afternoon to see how you're doing. Call my cell phone if you need to reach me in the meantime."

"I'll do that, thanks."

"Okay. Good night, then."

"Good night."

Kristin watched him disappear into the hall and listened for the sound of his door closing, her nerves no more settled now than if he'd gone. Then she grabbed a dorm shirt, fresh undies and a bottle of peach-scented body wash, and hurried into the bathroom.

Zach lay in bed, listening to the shower spray, aware of a clean, sweet fragrance that wasn't his soap wafting under his closed door…aware of the knot in his gut and his burgeoning arousal.

He fought with the stack of pillows beneath his head, then threw two of them on the floor and clicked off the muted TV sitting atop his bureau. He must have been insane to insist that she stay with him after she'd told him she and Chad were just friends. Not that he wanted to see her with the pretentious blowhard, but he'd depended on her relationship with Chad to keep her visit uncomplicated. Now, he'd be fighting his body's natural impulses the entire time she was here.

Scowling, Zach amended his thought. All right, he would've had to fight those impulses anyway. But it would've been a hell of a lot easier if he'd believed she was promised to someone else.

He heard her leave the bathroom and pad across the hall to the guest room, then softly shut the door.

Images from the past rolled through Zach's mind, waking up every blood vessel he owned, and leaving him with the disturbing knowledge that the attraction he'd felt for her as a teenager was even more powerful now that they were adults.

Planning to do anything about it? a little voice in his mind asked.

He almost laughed at the absurdity of the question. No, he didn't plan on doing anything about it. Smart men assuaged their physical needs without involvement or emotional baggage. And he'd been smart for a long time.

The ringing of the phone shattered Zach's sleep, and he fumbled for it beside his bed. He swore when he knocked his wristwatch on the floor. Snaring the receiver, he rolled onto his back again, his head sinking gratefully into his pillow. Though he cleared his throat, his voice was still thick with sleep when he spoke.

"Hello?"

The sharp, feminine voice on the line brought him quickly awake. "Where's my sister?"

"I—" Zach squinted at the lighted dial on his bedside clock. It was just breaking day. "Rachel?"

"Do you have anyone else's sister there with you?"

Zach swore under his breath, kicked back the sheet and rolled to a sitting position on the mattress. He rubbed the cleft between his brows, a headache already building. "Rachel, why don't I just give the phone to Kris and let the two of you talk?" *And what the hell time was it in Arizona anyway? Didn't the woman sleep?*

"Not just yet. We need to get something straight first."

"And what would that be?" he asked testily, pushing to his feet.

"Just this—Kristin's had enough pain because of you. She doesn't need any more. If you hurt her again, Zach, I swear—"

"Yeah, yeah, I know. You'll hunt me down like the dog I am. Well, forgive the hell out of me for not digging my own grave and throwing myself in long ago. For the record, I didn't exactly tap-dance my way through life after we broke up, either. But that probably never occurred to you."

"To be frank, it did occur to me. But I was too busy trying to piece my sister back together and take care of my mother to give it much thought."

"I'll get Kristin," he said coldly. "Delightful talking to you, as always."

Zach yanked open his door and strode across the hall, getting more ticked off by the moment. He was physically and mentally beat, hadn't slept worth a damn, and he didn't need a personal attack at 5:00 a.m. to start his day. He rapped at Kristin's door, waited for her hesitant, "Come in," then went inside.

The faint half light edging the miniblinds outlined her soft curves as she sat amid tangled sheets and pillows. For just a second, Zach felt himself sinking into the vulnerable intimacy of early morning, stirred by the sensual smells of perfume and feminine sleep.

Then he remembered the cordless phone he carried like an acid-tongued serpent in his hand, and went to her bedside. "It's for you," he said flatly. "Rachel the Compassionate. I'm going for a swim."

Kristin took the phone, her pulse kicking at the

shadowy sight of him in only a pair of dark shorts. Even his obvious anger and the strained conversation she'd overheard couldn't keep her attention from his broad shoulders and muscular legs.

Drawing a deep breath, she spoke into the phone. "Hi."

To Kristin's relief, Rachel's tone was soft and concerned. "Kris, I'm so sorry about your beautiful shop."

"Me, too."

"What are you going to do?"

"Rebuild, maybe. I'm not sure yet. That's why I'm here—to get some focus and perspective."

Too late, Kristin realized that her reply had opened the door to a discussion she didn't want to have. She closed her eyes.

Rachel didn't mince words about Kristin's staying with Zach when there was a perfectly beautiful guest room available to her in Arizona. By the time Kristin insisted that Rachel go to bed and get some sleep, she was too keyed up to go back to sleep herself.

Pulling on a T-shirt and sweatpants, she went to the kitchen to brew coffee for breakfast, then opened the blinds fronting the Atlantic. Zach was just leaving the choppy surf, the dark swim trunks he wore hugging his lean hips. Her heart took off running again, and a tug of arousal pulled behind her navel. There was no denying her attraction to him, despite their past. Hard work and Carolina sunshine had created a beautifully put-together man.

She was pouring coffee into two thick mugs when he surprised her by coming up the basement steps from the garage.

"Just me," he said, wiping a towel over his chest,

then draping it around his neck. "I showered down-stairs."

Kristin put a cup of coffee in his hand, trying not to look at the black hair covering his chest. "I'm sorry," she said as he leaned back against the bar and took a tentative sip.

His brows raised. "About what?"

"Rachel. She told me what she said to you."

"Yeah, well…it was a bad time for her back then." He paused. "It was a bad time for both of you."

Kristin nodded, not really wanting to revisit a past she couldn't change. "I checked the fridge. Do you want breakfast?"

"No, but thanks for making coffee. It's great." In spite of her changing the subject, he returned to the previous topic. "I really am sorry about your mom. I always liked her. I wish you'd told me back then, Kris."

Sometimes she wished she had, too. It might have made a difference in their lives. Although…would telling him sooner have prevented his betraying her after some other misunderstanding? She had no way of knowing.

Sliding onto one of the barstools, she cupped her hands around her mug. "My mom always liked you, too." Well, she had until Zach had torn her younger daughter's heart to shreds.

"I know, and I was grateful. She never looked at me the way other people did—like I had a switchblade in my boot and a pint of whiskey in my back pocket."

Kristin met his eyes. "Zach, a lot of that was in your mind. I think most people felt sorry for you."

"Wonderful. Pity for Hap Davis's welfare kid. Somehow that's worse." With an annoyed frown, he finished his coffee, then walked to the sink to rinse his cup. "I'd better change and get to work. Dan and I are meeting with Mrs. Hart at nine, and I need to take care of a few things before we talk with her."

"Then I'll see you back here later?"

"Hopefully, by six, but I can't promise you it won't be later. If I do finish early, we can go out for dinner. Do you like crab legs?"

"Only if they're dripping in butter," she returned, grinning.

Zach chuckled, his momentary irritation gone. "Then you'd better wear something washable, because we're going to get messy."

There was a warm, silly lilt in her heart when she walked him out onto the deck shortly afterward and said goodbye. But as it generally did when a reasonable distance separated them, reality reappeared quickly. It was a mistake to feel warm, lilting things for him. She was merely vacationing here for a few days, nothing more. Even if there were more…even if they didn't live three states away and live very different lives…trust was a difficult thing to mend once it was broken.

Lifting her sailboat to her lips, Kristin stared out at the blue-green Atlantic and blew softly, hoping her mother had been right.

Chapter 8

Later that morning, Kristin descended the long wooden stairs to the beach to walk the shoreline, determined to enjoy herself. She smiled at the tiny, lightning-quick crabs that burrowed to safety after being sloshed onto the beach by the waves, marveled at the gulls and pelicans winging over the water. This truly was a much different world than the one she knew. All around her, people played with their children and splashed in the surf, oblivious to anything else going on in the world.

She felt a twinge of longing as she gathered shells and watched twin toddlers race across the sand with their pails and shovels. The little boys couldn't have been older than three, their red swimming trunks drooping sweetly over their baby bellies. How wonderful it would be to have a child of her own.

She was still thinking about the twins when she walked back to Zach's beach house.

We'd have beautiful kids, Chad had said, and she wanted them badly. But there was no chemistry with Chad, no excitement. No breathless feeling of anticipation for a touch or a kiss…or that shivery joining in the dark. She'd had that once.

It hurt to know that someday she might have to settle for less.

When Zach didn't call by twelve-thirty, she fixed herself a sandwich and glass of milk for lunch. By three-thirty, she'd dusted furniture that hadn't needed dusting, taken a short nap on the deck, and baked a chocolate cake from a mix she'd found in his cupboard.

By five o'clock, she'd shed her black swimsuit for a yellow one-piece romper. Zach had said they might go out for dinner, but the more she considered the long hours he worked in the heat, the more she felt that eating here was best. He had all the fixings for grilled chicken salads—and they did have a chocolate cake for dessert. She smiled. If they stayed in this evening, they could watch the sunset together.

Niggling concerns began to creep in when there was no word from him by seven, and by nine-thirty, Kristin was beside herself with worry.

Striding to the kitchen phone, she dialed the number on the Davis Construction calendar hanging beside it. Her heart pounded as she waited through half a dozen rings. If something had gone wrong, someone at the trailer would be able to tell her. Providing anyone was there at this hour.

A man with a warm Carolina drawl picked up the receiver. "Davis Construction."

Kristin willed herself to calm down. "Hello. This is—I'm a friend of Mr. Davis's. Is he there?"

"Just a minute. I'll check." The man covered the mouthpiece and called out. He didn't cover it well enough. "You here? It's a woman." After a short pause, he said, "Naw, a different voice from the one who called yesterday. *Nice* voice."

There was a click, then Zach was on the line. "Davis."

"Zach, hi," she said hesitantly. "I guess I got you at a bad time."

His low groan was full of apology. "Oh hell, Kris, I'm sorry. I'm up to my ears in trouble here. I meant to call you earlier, but I got so involved with— What time is it?" he asked, then answered himself. "Damn. It's after nine. Look, I can probably finish in a half hour or so—"

"No, don't rush on my account," she cut in, trying to ignore her disappointment. "I was just a little worried when I didn't hear from you." She forced a laugh. "I kept picturing you in traction somewhere."

After a long pause, he said soberly, "I'm not used to checking in with anyone."

In the background, another male voice yelled that he was heading home. Covering the phone, Zach called back, "Thanks for hanging those cupboards. See you tomorrow," then resumed their conversation. Though he sounded interested when he asked about her day, Kristin knew that his had been long, and her phone call was making it longer.

"I had fun. The beach is glorious. But we can talk about that tomorrow. I'll let you get back to work."

"You're okay?"

"I'm fine. See you in the morning. I'll show you the shells I found."

''Looking forward to it,'' he said warmly. ''Good night.''

''Good night.''

Kristin replaced the handset, then walked slowly to her room to change for bed. There was no reason to feel down, she told herself sensibly. He'd told her at the outset that he worked twelve- to sixteen-hour days in the summer months. In fact, that was one of the selling points for this trip. They wouldn't be together a lot, which meant they wouldn't be constantly battling the chemistry between them.

She was in bed, listening through the window screens to the waves breaking on the shore when she finally realized why that low feeling persisted. The man who'd answered the phone had said another woman had phoned for Zach the previous day.

Who was she, and what did she mean to Zach? *How much* did she mean to him?

Kristin rolled onto her side and tried to put it out of her mind. Silly, class-ring-on-a-gold-chain jealousies were natural, given their past. They didn't mean anything.

She was still telling herself that when she drifted into an uneasy sleep.

A loud noise shattered Kristin's sleep, and she sat upright in bed. Instantly on edge, she mentally retraced her steps before retiring. She'd locked the doors, locked the windows, pulled the blinds—

Then she caught the faint aroma of freshly brewed coffee, and smiled. No self-respecting thief would stop to make coffee while he was burglarizing a house. Zach was home.

Zipping herself into her long hunter green robe,

Kristin went out to the living room. She halted abruptly in the doorway.

A warm, gentle feeling welled up inside of her as her gaze rested on the softly snoring giant on the couch.

Zach was stretched out full-length, his neck and dark head at an awkward angle on the turquoise-and-coral throw pillows, his booted feet dangling off the edge of the sofa and scraping the floor. He held a coffee mug between his hands, and that mug rested precariously on his flat stomach.

Kristin moved quietly to retrieve the mug, noting the thick binder full of papers that had fallen between the sofa and coffee table—probably the sound she'd heard. As gently as she could, she eased the mug from Zach's hands and put it on the table. The cup was still warm.

A tingle of attraction moved through her. From the black hair falling over his forehead to the dark stubble on his jaw, to his booted feet, he was everything a man should be. Kristin watched his black T-shirt rise and fall with his deep respirations. The insecure boy she'd known was gone, replaced by the confident, mature man he'd become.

Her gaze returned to his feet. And before she could decide if it was advisable or not, she'd picked up the heavy binder and placed it on the table, then dropped to her knees to loosen his laces and cautiously slip off his boots. Kristin pulled gently at his damp white socks to give his toes more room, feeling her heart soften as she looked again at his slumbering features.

Did she dare adjust the pillows under his head? He was bound to wake up with a stiff neck if he stayed in that position all night, wasn't he?

Creeping silently to his side, she bent down.

His gray eyes opened.

Jolted, she stepped back, heat flooding her face. "I'm sorry. I didn't mean to wake you. I just— You looked so uncomfortable lying there like that, I thought I should—"

Smiling tiredly, Zach sat up and pulled a pillow onto his lap, then planted his elbows there and rubbed his face. "No problem. Thanks for caring. I didn't plan to fall asleep... just wanted to rest my eyes for a while. Guess I zonked out."

"Guess so," she replied, still feeling awkward. "Did things go well with Mrs. Hart?"

"For the most part. She's hanging in there with us, but now she wants the floor plan changed. That's what I was working on when you phoned—cost estimates for the extra lumber and materials we'll need. I still have a few calls to make when the building supply houses open in the morning."

"You're being incredibly understanding about the changes she wants."

He released a dry laugh. "No, I'm being incredibly greedy. I told you she has rich friends who might need a contractor some day. I'm willing to jump through a few hoops to keep her happy."

Kristin returned his smile, thinking that a simple grin shouldn't make her feel so bubbly and joyful inside. "I should go back to bed and let you get some sleep," she said. "I imagine tomorrow will be another early day for you."

"Unfortunately."

"Feeling like a hamster on a little wheel?"

He grinned again. "It's the only way to build a business."

"I suppose so. Well…good night."

"'Night, Kris. Sweet dreams."

"You, too."

When Kristin had disappeared behind the guest room's closed door, Zach released a long, pent-up breath. He'd woke up the second he felt her take away his coffee mug. Then he'd lain there with all of his senses keyed as she'd fiddled with his laces and slipped off his boots.

He'd never dreamed that *toes* could be an erogenous zone. Grateful he'd had a pillow handy, he took it off his lap and tossed it on the far corner of the sofa. Then he doused the lights, went to his room, and flopped into his big, empty bed.

Every time he looked at her, he wanted her. And if his radar was working even a little, Kris was having some of the same feelings. But she was here to clear her head, and he knew the primary forces fueling his desire were memories and a long period of abstinence. He had to stay away from her.

It was going to be a long, miserable night.

The night was longer and more miserable than he expected. At six o'clock, bleary-eyed and still needy, Zach tapped on Kristin's door to say goodbye.

"Come in," she said clearly, and he wondered if she'd slept badly, too.

Poking his head inside, he smiled as she sat up and pulled the sheet to her chest. In the faint light of morning, her hair was tousled, and her Yankees dorm shirt hung off her right shoulder. She tugged it back up.

"Leaving already?" she asked. "Seems like you just got home."

"You know what they say—no rest for the

wicked." The fresh smells of peaches and salt air permeated the room, making his battered nerve endings vibrate. "We'll go out for dinner tonight. For sure." Her smile started a tickle, low in his stomach.

"I'd like that."

"Good. I would, too." He nodded at the mayonnaise jar full of shells on her nightstand, and against all sane thought, walked to her bedside. "These are what you found, huh?"

Lifting the jar, he tipped it to the sunlight coming through the blinds. "Pretty shells—crummy container."

"I know. When I get back home, I'll put them into one of the apothecary jars I have at my…shop." She stopped abruptly, and tears welled in her eyes. Then she said in a falsely bright tone, "Well, maybe not."

Torn, Zach looked down at her. He wanted to hold her, but that was a bad idea. He knew how quickly comforting could become something else. It had happened before, and she'd pretty much told him she didn't want any more of it. As long as she kept up a brave front, he could keep his distance. "It'll all work out."

"Will it? I don't know."

"But I do," he said sincerely. "You'll rebuild, and your new shop will be everything the old one was, and more. Because this time, you'll choose everything from the floor coverings, to the ceilings, to the design and exterior of the building. And you'll find pieces even more beautiful than the ones you lost. Prettier vases, prettier dolls, prettier—"

Zach swore beneath his breath as the tears he'd tried to discourage splashed over her lower lashes. A moment later, he was holding her while she sobbed and wondering why he hadn't been bright enough to just change the subject.

"I hate this!" she sobbed. "I thought I was finished crying!"

"It's okay."

"No, it's not. Crying doesn't accomplish a thing. It's stupid and weak."

Zach wrapped her more tightly in his arms, feeling a depth of compassion he hadn't felt in a long time. But like her mini breakdown after the fire, she pulled herself together quickly. He was almost disappointed when she did.

"I tried my architectural skills yesterday while you were gone," she said, daubing at her eyes with the tissue he handed her from the box on the nightstand. "I'm no threat to the professionals, but I do have some ideas someone might be able to improve upon."

"If you have a starting point, the rest is easy."

She released a disbelieving laugh, and reaching out, he wiped a stray tear away. "Have some faith."

"I do. Most days."

He knew what she meant. He'd had days like that, too. Days when he'd wanted to grow up, get out, make a better life for himself. Now here he was, moderately successful and living in an oceanfront beach house... and sitting inches away from the most desirable woman he'd ever known. She turned him inside out. Even with tears in her eyes and a red nose.

That gut-gnawing attraction moved through him again. Worse, he saw the same awareness coalescing in her eyes. It was the touching, the holding...the memories. For several seconds, they held each other's gazes. Then, sighing and calling himself a fool, Zach pushed to his feet and backed away. If he did anything about this, they'd both regret it afterward.

"I'd better hit the trail. Dan and the guys will be wondering where I am. See you around six."

"I'll be here," she said with a tight smile.

Fifteen minutes later, Zach strode inside the already sweltering, two-room trailer, kicked a pair of sandy work boots away from the door, then went to his desk and collapsed into his office chair. The desktop was still strewn with floor plans and estimates, the paper mess tenting his coffee cup. It all swam before his eyes.

All he could see was Kristin looking so sweet and sexy in that bed. All he could feel was his body rising willingly to the occasion. He let out a wistful blast of air. He was learning more than he ever wanted to know about restraint these days. Thank God they'd be going back to Pennsylvania soon.

The door swung open. Zach glanced up as Dan Perkins lumbered inside, letting the screen door bang shut behind him. He looked rough around the edges, eyes bloodshot, but not from booze. Dan was a six-foot-four, three hundred pound tee-totaler whose tastes ran to cheeseburgers and pizza, and who was nearly as dedicated to the company as Zach was.

Dan pulled his hands down over two days' worth of whiskers and stared soberly. "Don't you sleep at all?"

"I got a few hours. You?"

"Six. Why in hell do you look better'n me?"

Zach chuckled and started straightening his desk. "I shaved."

Ambling into the small kitchen, his foreman pulled

coffee and filters from a marred cupboard. "I can't imagine you gettin' any sleep at all with a woman living in your house."

Zach stiffened, but kept his voice casual. "You slept and there's a woman living in your house, too."

"No, there's a wife living in my house. Big difference. By the time Patty gets the kids to bed at night, she's ready to go to sleep, not to bed." He grinned brashly then, his whiskers bristling. "But that's okay. The kids'll grow up someday, then we'll have some time for each other again."

Zach couldn't be that open about his life. Fleeting and inconsequential as his relationships were, they were private. He particularly wouldn't talk about Kristin because she... He froze for an instant, then finished his surprising thought. Because she meant too much to him.

Gathering the scattered papers, he clicked on the computer to his right and forced a grin, while thoughts of her knotted his gut all over again. "You know what turns me on, Danny boy," he said. "Oak flooring and vaulted ceilings." The screen came up, icons bright. "Now let's see if we can find those brass fixtures Mrs. Hart's so hot to have."

Kristin winced as Chad's voice on the phone line slid upward in disbelief. "Where are you calling from? I don't recognize the number in the caller ID window."

"I'm in North Carolina. I'm staying with Zach for a few days."

Chad fell silent. When he spoke again, his tone was cool and controlled. "I see. Have you completely lost your mind?"

"It's not what you think," she hurried to say. "I needed to get away for a while after the fire, and since he was coming back here to take care of a problem, he invited me to come along. It was a friendly gesture, nothing more."

"Right."

"Chad, I don't want to debate this. I phoned to see if there was anything new on the fire. I would have called the firehouse, but I didn't think anyone would be there to answer the phone." The men of Wisdom's volunteer fire department worked at other jobs until an emergency arose.

"You called because of the fire? That's it? You weren't even planning to let me know where you were? I've been worried sick about you for the past two days."

"I—I'm sorry," she answered, guilt creeping in.

"Didn't you realize that if you disappeared right after a suspected arson, I might think you'd been harmed?"

Kristin squeezed her eyes shut, knowing her oversight had been inexcusable. "No, I didn't even consider it. I really am sorry. The trip came up so suddenly I guess I wasn't thinking about much else. *Is* there any news on the fire?"

"No, nothing yet. The fire marshal hopes to be here in a few days."

"Good. I really need some answers." She softened her tone, trying to banish his down-in-the-dumps mood. "How are you?"

"Busy. Had another break-in at Anna Mae's house last night."

That jolted her. "You're joking."

"Unfortunately, no. One of the neighbors reported

seeing lights on and called us, so Larry and I went over. We found Harlan Greene going through her knickknacks. He said he just wanted a frog or two to remember her by.''

Recalling the sadness in Harlan's eyes the day he came into her shop, Kristin felt a rush of sympathy. ''Oh, Chad, you're not planning to bring charges, are you?''

''I don't know,'' he answered in a troubled voice. ''Technically, it wasn't breaking and entering. He had a key. But the house doesn't belong to him. It belongs to Mrs. Arnett.''

A sudden, unwelcome thought occurred to Kristin. ''You don't think Harlan was the one who—''

''—broke in before? I considered it, but, no. He's such a nice old coot, I suspect he would've stayed to give you first aid if he was the one who collided with you on the stairs. Besides, I asked him, and he said no. I think he was telling the truth.'' The coolness returned to his voice as he changed the subject. ''When are you coming home?''

''In a day or two. As soon as Zach finishes his business here.''

''Good,'' he murmured, then added in an even gentler voice, ''I miss you.''

Kristin suppressed a sigh. She didn't want him to miss her. ''Have you seen Mary Alice since the auction?''

''No. Why would I?''

Obviously because she was his date for the dinner cruise next Saturday night. But if there was nothing there, there was nothing there. ''Chad, I'll see you when I get back. I'm sorry you were worried. Take care.''

''You take care, too,'' he replied, but his words carried a heavier meaning.

Kristin hung up the phone, thoughts of Harlan overshadowing her frustration with Chad. Sometimes life was so unfair. It made her sad to think of the old, bow-tied gentleman choosing a frog from Anna Mae's collection...a small remembrance of a woman he'd loved and would never see again.

Her gaze slid to the coffee table where Anna Mae's journals were stacked. She felt their pull. Moments later, she was in a chair on the deck, sunglasses on, and reading.

The first entry was penned midway through Anna Mae's tour in the tropics, though it wasn't with the Peace Corps as Chad had said. She'd been with missionary friends in the jungles of Panama. And the reason she'd begun writing was...Paul. Another of the volunteers, he was a few years older than she, and was ''...*the most extraordinary man I've ever known. Dedicated and caring, even when he's exhausted from the heat and the brutality of what we see here. I am completely in love with him.*''

A sentimental warmth filled her heart as Kristin continued to read, filling her mind with the lovers' adventures. Her throat knotted when Anna Mae and Paul lost some of the ''friends'' they'd come to help to fevers and other illnesses. But it was also wonderful seeing Anna Mae for the first time as a vibrant young woman in her twenties, so full of caring and compassion as she worked in the oppressive heat alongside doctors and nurses. The love in Anna Mae's lyrical prose was never so apparent as when she mentioned Paul. He was her world, her soul mate. And from the simple gifts he gave her—a jungle flower, a colorful feather, butterscotch candies from home—Kristin knew that he'd loved Anna Mae as well.

But as Kristin continued to read, a feeling of dread crept over her. Anna Mae had died in her late-sixties, never having married. What had happened? Why hadn't she and Paul had the life they'd dreamed of? Why had there been no babies with blue eyes and cornsilk hair?

She flipped through the pages. When she reached the terrible entry that answered her questions, tears welled in her eyes.

Cancer. Inoperable. Terminal.

Chapter 9

Footsteps sounded on the wooden stairs. Snapping the journal shut, Kristin set it aside and wiped her eyes. She rose as a slender woman with shoulder-length, pale-blond hair reached the top step, then abruptly halted on the deck. Her startled look said Kristin was a surprise.

Recovering, she came forward, poised, slim and extremely pretty in crisp khaki slacks and a white designer top that showed off her tan. Sunlight touched her hair and the fine gold necklace at her throat.

"Hi," she said warmly. "I didn't expect to find anyone here." She glanced toward the door. "Is Zach in? I phoned the trailer a few days ago, and Dan said he'd be out of town for a while."

Her easy familiarity brought a faint twinge of jealousy. Kristin mustered a smile. "He came back to take care of a problem, but he'll be leaving again soon. I'd be glad to take a message, Ms.—?"

"Michaels." Shifting the trendy plastic bag she carried to her left hand, she extended her right one to briefly clasp Kristin's. "But, please, call me Stephanie."

"Kristin. I'm a friend of Zach's."

The woman took in Kristin's auburn hair and dark eyes, then her swimsuit and bare feet. "That's nice," she said with what looked like a resigned smile. "Everyone needs friends." She handed Kristin the bag with the designer logo. "Would you see that Zach gets this? When I was packing and cleaning out my apartment, I found a sweatshirt he left there a few months ago. Guess he never got around to missing it."

The disconcerting image of Zach and Stephanie together made it difficult to keep smiling, but Kristin managed. "Sounds like you're moving."

"Actually, I'm on my way to the airport now." Her gaze clouded. "My dad's not doing very well, so I asked for a transfer back to San Diego. The airline I work for has offices there."

Kristin experienced a swell of sympathy. She could relate. "It's great that your company can do that for you. I remember how important it was for me to be with my mom during her illness."

"Is she all right now?"

Kristin shook her head. "No. She passed away."

"Oh. I'm so sorry," Stephanie murmured, and Kristin knew she meant it.

"Me, too. I hope your dad will be okay."

"He has to be," she said working up a new smile. "He's my best friend." She glanced behind her. "I'd better go before I miss my plane."

"Bye. Have a safe flight."

"Thanks. And thanks for giving Zach the package."

She hadn't descended more than two steps when she turned around again. "Kristin?" she said hesitantly. "I...I want to say something, but I'm not sure I should."

A feeling of apprehension moved through her. It was obvious that what Stephanie had to say would be upsetting—and the only subject they had in common was Zach. "What is it?"

"Don't fall for him."

"I beg your pardon?"

"Don't fall for Zach. After a few dates, he'll back away and you'll end up wondering what you did to scare him off. The second any woman tries to get too close—and I've known a few—he buries himself in his work."

The weight on her chest made it hard for Kristin to affect a careless tone. "Thanks for the warning, but I'm just an old friend from Pennsylvania who's taking advantage of his hospitality for a few days."

"Good." Brow lining, Stephanie nodded to the bag she'd given Kristen. "To be honest, I've known I had that for a very long time. I'd just hoped that he'd come back sometime to pick it up."

Kristin didn't know what to say, other than to echo the woman's "goodbye." She couldn't lie and say that she, too, wished Zach had returned for the shirt. Because then he might have looked more closely at Stephanie Michaels's beautiful face and wide, clear eyes, and...

And he might have reconsidered a relationship with Stephanie that would've made Kristin's visit here impossible.

Blocking out everything that thought implied, Kristin hurried out of the sunshine and into the air-conditioned house. She went to Zach's room.

Though she'd glanced inside the night she'd arrived, she hadn't actually gone in. Now as she looked around, it struck her that the bed's heavily bolstered, cherry head- and footboard and matching bureaus were vastly different from the generic groupings in the rest of the house. This wasn't part of his rental package. Navy, white and burgundy drapes in a muted leaf design were pulled back from the patio door leading to the deck, and a rectangle of sunlight spilled onto the coordinating spread covering his king-size bed. A photo of Zach and his aunt Etta sat on his dresser beside one of two brass lamps, and a bold geometric print hung over the bed.

It was a beautiful room, strikingly masculine and well suited to Zach's personality. But something else in the room commanded Kristin's attention even more than the furnishings.

Placing the bag at the foot of his bed, she crossed to the easel standing in a corner to the right of his nightstand—an easel holding a large, detailed charcoal drawing of a dramatic beach house on stilts. Surrounded on three sides by a wraparound deck, it featured additional, multileveled descending decks, a steeply pitched roof and a front fashioned entirely of wood beams and glass.

She stroked the textured paper, her heart beginning to beat fast again. If this home were for someone else, wouldn't it be in his office with the other drawings and blueprints she'd seen?

This had to be Zach's dream house…a home he would build here in the Carolinas, further cementing his roots here. She felt her chest tighten. It was such a large house for a man Stephanie had implied would spend his life alone. Without a wife, without children…without love.

"Like it?"

Kristin turned in surprise to see Zach braced against the doorway, and she flushed guiltily at being caught in his room. It amazed her that she hadn't sensed him there. Now that she knew, the air seemed to crackle with energy. Maybe because his slow, silent appraisal of her said he liked what he saw. Her face, her bathing suit…her legs. The temperature inched up several degrees.

"Yes, I like it very much," she answered, her pulse quickening. "You're early."

"I'm not staying. I just stopped in to pick up a file from my office."

Zach pushed away from the door frame, and Kristin motioned to the shopping bag at the foot of his bed. "I wasn't being nosy. I just came in to drop off your package and couldn't leave without taking a closer look at the house. Yours?"

"Someday," he said, picking up the bag. His black hair was attractively wind-tossed, the dark green T-shirt and soft jeans he wore hugging his shoulders and hips.

He frowned curiously as he pulled a navy blue hooded sweatshirt from the bag. "Where'd this come from?"

She should move, Kristin told herself. She should leave this quickly heating, slowly shrinking room. "Isn't it yours?"

"Yes, but I haven't seen it for a while." He tossed the sweatshirt back on the bed and looked up, silently questioning.

"You left it at Stephanie Michaels's apartment. She tried to reach you at the trailer but you were out of town." Kristin paused, gauging his reaction. "She's leaving for San Diego today."

"Oh." Was that a flicker of regret she saw in his eyes? "Dan said someone had called. Guess that clears up the mystery."

"She seems nice. I think she liked you a lot."

"She is nice, and I liked her, too." He picked up the sweatshirt and walked to his closet.

"Can I ask what happened?" Kristin asked, wondering if he would answer. He hadn't shared anything of a personal nature since they'd reconnected.

Zach located a stray hanger among the neatly hung clothing in his closet and slid the sweatshirt onto it. "She was looking for something permanent. I wasn't. There's no room in my life for that right now."

"So you've said," Kristin replied soberly. "I'm still surprised that you didn't give it a chance. I suspect most men would have a hard time walking away from a woman that beautiful."

He hung the shirt and shut the louvered door. "I'm not most men," he said, turning back to her.

No argument there.

Something flickered through his expression, something that mimicked the air between them. Warm, thick, electric. He walked toward her.

"You're right," he said quietly. "She *is* beautiful. She's also polished, intelligent and witty. But...I've always been partial to women with auburn hair. Women with a more relaxed approach to life. Stephanie's too...perfect. Maybe it's because of her job with the airline. But it's important to her that her nails, hair, jewelry, clothes are all perfect, all the time."

They were only inches apart now, the walls closing in on them. "Perfection is a turnoff?"

Zach shook his head, his gray eyes dark and his voice low as he held her gaze. "No, it wasn't a turnoff. The truth is, there was no turn-*on*. There was no snap, no sizzle. No bells ringing, no blood rushing..."

She stopped breathing as Zach took her hand and pressed it to his chest. "Feel that?" he whispered. His warm fingers stroked the back of her hand while his heart thudded solidly beneath her palm.

Oh, yes, she felt that. With every scrape of his callused fingers, her nerve endings pulsed crazily beneath her skin.

"There was none of this with her. If I ever do commit to another woman, I want it all. Every bit of it. I want to look at her and feel the floodgates open." His next sentence was barely audible. "I want to look at her and feel my belly turn to Jell-O."

Kristin nodded, half-afraid that the scant movement would break the moment—more afraid that it wouldn't. When she spoke, her voice was so low and shaky she scarcely recognized it. "I suppose once you've known that kind of chemistry, it's...it's difficult to settle for less."

"It's not difficult," Zach rasped. "It's impossible."

Floodgates opened everywhere. Zach descended upon her hungrily, his kiss all pent-up passion and earthy need. In a flash, Kristin's arms were round his neck, and she was answering his kiss with a need of her own. She reveled in the stroking of his tongue, in the wonderful feel of him in her arms. And it must have been right, because those nagging voices that had once warned her away from him allowed her to float on pure sensation without interrupting.

Kristin felt him grow hard against her, felt the heat of his breath as he continued to gulp harsh kisses from her and work her straps down over her shoulders, work black Lycra down over her breasts.

She expelled a tattered sigh as he filled his hands with her softness, then slid her suit down farther, stealing her breath and her will. Slowly, heated lips drinking eagerly from each other again, they moved toward his bed, knees bumping, even that small contact thrilling their senses.

Kristin moved her hands to the waistband of his jeans and found his belt buckle. They were older now. There would be no juvenile fumbling. They would link and love and explore every avenue of pleasure they'd denied themselves since that tingling kiss in his truck.

Fingers trembling, she dispensed with the buckle and turned her attention to the metal button behind it.

"Yo, Zach! You 'bout ready? It's hot in that damn truck!"

Stunned they sprang back from each other, Kristin drawing a sharp breath, and Zach's eyes widening in shock.

"Thought you were comin' right back out!"

Zach's mind swam. "I—I am!" he shouted back, astonished that he'd forgotten Dan was waiting. "Grab a Pepsi from the fridge! I'm still looking for those prints!"

Galvanized into action, he grabbed the stretchy fabric at Kristin's waist and tried to tug it back up. He flushed when the neckline got stuck under her breasts, and she shoved his hands away.

"I'm sorry," he whispered in a rush. "I have to go."

"I know." She slid her arms through her straps and pulled her suit up. "I'll see you for dinner."

Pecking a quick kiss on her forehead, Zach hurried to his office, hoping to God that Dan wouldn't walk into the hall before he pulled himself together.

Dear God, he was losing his mind. One look at her standing beside his bed in that swimsuit that hid nothing, and all he could think of was peeling her out of it and pinning her to his mattress. Then another thought occurred to him, and it was a bad one.

He'd just told her that he'd see her for dinner. And dinner was off.

Dan glanced up from popping the tab on his soft drink when Zach entered the living room, finger combing his hair with his free hand. His big, burly foreman paused in the act of bringing the Pepsi to his lips, stared for a long second, then started to chuckle. Zach felt himself color all over again.

"So vaulted ceilings and hardwood floors are the only things that turn you on, huh, Romeo?"

Zach stabbed an index finger toward him as he stalked past to snatch his keys from the bar. "Not another word if you want a paycheck this week."

Dan's green eyes twinkled beneath his bushy brows. "Fine by me, but if I were you, I'd do somethin' about that danglin' belt buckle."

Zach glanced down in irritation, then scowled as he hitched his belt tight and buckled himself up again. He swore beneath his breath when he realized there was also a slowly departing lump in his jeans that hadn't been there when he walked inside a few minutes ago. Wonderful.

Suddenly, Dan's attention moved to a spot behind Zach, and his look grew respectful. When Zach turned around, he was startled to see Kristin enter the room. He would've thought she'd hide out until Dan left to avoid any more embarrassment.

"Afternoon, ma'am," Dan said deferentially.

Now chastely covered by a white beach robe, Kristin mustered a smile and returned the greeting. But her cheeks were pink, and there was a raw-looking red spot beside her mouth that could only be whisker burn. Zach damned himself all over again.

"You dropped this in the hall," she said quietly, handing him a sheet of paper. "It looked important."

"It is. Thanks." He hazarded another glance at Dan. His foreman stood grinning like a lunatic, obviously delighted with the situation.

"I'm Dan Perkins, ma'am," he said heartily, and extended a meaty hand. "I think we spoke on the phone last night."

Blushing prettily, Kristin clasped his hand. "Kristin Chase. And yes, I think we did. It's nice to meet you, Mr. Perkins."

"Dan," his foreman corrected her. "How're you enjoyin' your stay?"

Zach jammed the truck's keys into Dan's palm and nudged him toward the door. "She's enjoying it just fine. Start the truck and turn on the air-conditioning. I'll be right out."

"Nice seein' you, ma'am," he called in amusement as Zach propelled him through the screen door. His next sentence made Zach cringe. "I'll try to speed up the meetin' so the boss here can be home by ten."

When the door had banged shut and Dan was out of earshot, Zach turned slowly to meet Kristin's gaze. The hurt and confusion in her eyes made him feel lousy.

"That was the other reason I stopped in today."

"Dinner's off?"

He nodded. "I got a call this afternoon from a guy over in Manteo who's interested in a beach house similar to one we put up for a friend of his. If the price is right."

"You're starting something new?"

It sounded like a criticism, and Zach grew defensive. "I know I came back to settle another matter, but when an opportunity like this comes up, I have to grab it."

"The meeting can't be rescheduled?"

"The client and I are both pressed for time right now. He's leaving the island in a few days, and I have to get back to Etta's. I told him we'd see him tonight to work out the figures."

Kristin drew a calming breath. All right, this was his business and he had to see that it thrived. She understood that perfectly. But suddenly Stephanie's words about Zach burying himself in work came back to her, and she wondered if this new client was a way to put distance between them after they'd nearly made love. After she'd stupidly given her heart free rein in a situation that had no future.

Tears stung the backs of her eyes, and she glanced away. "Then I guess I'll see you when I see you."

Cupping her chin, Zach turned her face back to him. "You're upset."

"No."

"Yes."

Kristin jerked away. "All right, I'm upset. Five minutes ago, you were prepared to blow off all of your obligations to strip me naked. You even managed to forget that Dan was waiting for you outside. Now you're pressed for time?"

"You have to know that I didn't plan for any of that to happen. I came back for the file, and when I saw you in my room, I just—" He stopped, pinched the bridge of his nose. "Can we talk about this later? If I don't leave soon, Dan will be back in here grinning like a damn loon again. I'll see you as soon as I can. Okay?"

She nodded, but she wasn't certain she'd be here when he got back. Beneath her raw emotions, she suddenly realized why she was so upset. And it had more to do with Stephanie's insights than it did with a broken dinner date. "Look, just ignore what I said," she sighed. "That was frustration and embarrassment talking."

"If it's any consolation, I'm feeling some of that, too."

It wasn't, but she said, "I know" anyway.

"I'll see you later, then," he repeated as he opened the door and stepped out onto the deck.

"Sure," she answered. "Have a good meeting."

For the next few hours, Kristin fought with herself over what to do. This arrangement of theirs wasn't working. She tried to lose her low mood in the second journal, unwilling to read any more about Anna Mae's devastation over losing Paul.

But when she came across a startling, yet touching entry about her own mother, Kristin dissolved into tears. Shutting the journal, she went to the phone to call the airline for departure times and available flights. There was as much turmoil here as there was in Wisdom. She needed to go home.

As for Zach...

Stephanie was right. His first priority was his work, consciously or unconsciously, and anything else came in a distant second. That wasn't the kind of man she wanted to fall in love with. And if she didn't get away from him very soon, that could very well happen.

She was packing her bags when she heard the door open and bang shut, followed by heavy footsteps, several curious thuds and the rattle of paper and plastic.

Zipping her luggage shut, she carried it into the living room and braced herself for the discussion they were about to have. Zach was at the kitchen bar, unloading grocery bags.

She stopped dead in her tracks when she saw the carton of fresh strawberries and the thick plaid blanket beside it.

"Hi," she said, blocking the memories those strawberries evoked. She took her carry-on to the door and set it down. "I didn't expect you back so soon. Did your meeting go well?"

Zach stared at her luggage for a long beat. Without commenting on it, he carried the berries to the sink. "I bailed a little early, but yeah, it went well." He turned on the tap, rinsed the berries and dropped them into a bowl. "I figured if Dan wants to be a partner some day, he needs experience in the financial end of the business."

He finished and turned around, his expression grave. "I also thought that if we were going to roast hot dogs on the beach tonight, I should gather some wood and set things up while I could still see. But it looks like you're going somewhere."

He'd left his meeting so they could picnic on the beach?

A hope she knew she shouldn't be feeling stepped up her pulse. Kristin glanced through the screen door. Outside, the sky was taking on the midnight blue that preceded darkness, but stars had yet to appear. "You...gathered wood for a fire?"

He snagged a paper towel from the holder to his left, dried his hands, and tossed the towel into the nearby wastebasket. "Yep." Grimly, he took in her gray sweatpants and navy T-shirt. "It doesn't look like you're waiting for a taxi," he observed. "Do we have time for this?"

Time. There was that word again. "My flight leaves at ten tomorrow morning. I need to go home, Zach. I need to start rebuilding my life."

Nodding, he carried the berries to the bar. After a moment, he motioned to everything he'd assembled. "So. Should I put all this stuff away? I know it's not the seafood buffet I promised, and I know this afternoon was a disaster, but..." He stared blankly and opened his hands, indicating that there was nothing he could do about that. "Should I put it away?"

Kristin shook her head. He'd cut his meeting short to spend time with her—to make amends. She wouldn't let herself wonder if guilt or something more meaningful was the motivating force behind it. She only knew that her heart felt lighter than it had for hours, and that Zach wasn't as rigid about his priorities as his blond visitor had suggested.

"Don't put it away," she said quietly. "I'd like very much to have a picnic on the beach with you."

An hour later, their flame-seared hot dogs were a memory, and she was telling him about the entries in Anna Mae's journals while Zach roasted more marshmallows. He was crouched before the fire, several yards from the blanket they'd spread in the cove-shaped dunes below his house. Overhead, the black sky was littered with stars, and beyond the sandy beach, frothy waves broke on the shoreline.

Zach glanced back at her, his voice low. "Anna Mae left gifts for your mother? Anonymously?"

Kristin nodded, feeling her throat knot, but glad to be telling someone. Glad to be telling him. "Rachel and I used to find them beside the door. She always left them early in the morning, before anyone was awake. Sometimes there'd be a bouquet of bright, pretty flowers. Sometimes, a small box of candy, or a poem. Little things like Paul gave her when they were together in Panama."

Tears stung her eyes. "I guess in Anna Mae's mind, there was some sort of common denominator between Paul's cancer and my mother's, and Anna Mae wanted to do something kind for her."

"You're probably right," Zach said quietly. "She was a good woman. Even to me." He lifted the marsh-mallow from the fire, then came to the blanket and sank down beside her. "Want this?"

"No, two's my limit. Zach, what did you mean, Anna Mae was good to you, too?"

Zach popped the marshmallow into his mouth, then threw the stick, javelin-style, into the flames. He wiped his fingers on his jeans. "She pulled my fanny out of the fire when I was a kid and really needed a friend."

Firelight flickered over his rugged features, touching his perfect mouth and strong throat…the vee of chest hair visible in the open placket of his knit shirt.

"Anna Mae befriended you?"

Zach nodded. "Guess she didn't write about my little scrape with the law in her journals."

Kristin blinked. "She might have, but I didn't see anything about it. What happened?"

"It was right after my dad and I came back to town—I was about fifteen. I needed some decent clothes for school, and I didn't have any money or a job. So I shoplifted a pair of jeans. Funny," he added wryly, "we always had booze in the house, but food and clothes were no-shows."

He took the bowl of strawberries and a container of whipped cream out of the cooler. "Anyway, the manager of the store turned me in to the cops. I was only at the station a minute when Anna Mae jumped up from her desk and came to my rescue. She talked Chief Nance into letting me off with a warning, bought the jeans for me and let me work off my debt doing yard work for her that summer. But first, she took me aside and chewed me out royally. She knew how much my dad's escapades humiliated me, and she looked me right in the eyes and said I'd turn out the same way if I didn't shape up."

Kristin's heart softened for the boy he'd been.

"Actually," Zach went on with a slight smile, "I didn't even work that hard. She kept stopping me to feed me sandwiches and lemonade. I'd probably have a juvenile record now if it weren't for her."

"I never knew about that."

"I'm glad. It wasn't one of my shining moments." He looked at her again, a new memory in his eyes. "I didn't have a lot of those when we were together either, did I? Driving off like a hothead…getting trashed to the gills."

"Zach—"

"No, let me finish. For a long time, I tried to justify what I did by insisting that you shared the blame. But that was a lie. When Gretchen showed up, I told myself that you and I were through and you wouldn't give a damn. But I knew it would hurt you. Maybe that's why I did it."

He gestured to the strawberries, his voice dropping to a murmur. "That's why I brought these tonight. We cared about each other once. It was one of the best times of my life. When we were together, I felt like I was worth something—that if someone as sweet and decent as you are thought I had potential, than maybe I did." He slid the strawberries closer to her. "Tonight, I wanted to bring back a few nice memories."

Touched, Kristin met his eyes in the waning light of the fire, felt a warm breeze ruffle her hair. "That's ancient history. We're friends now."

"Good." Zach leaned over to kiss her softly, and there was so much gentleness in it, Kristin felt a knot form in her throat. Then he dipped two strawberries into the cream, and handed one to her. "A toast?"

"A toast with strawberries?" she said, laughing. Then, "Okay. To friendship," and bumped hers to his.

"To friendship." Zach fed her, then opened for the berry she slipped into his mouth. They chewed and smiled.

Then by unspoken agreement, they leaned forward again for another kiss, maybe because the moment required more than strawberries to seal it. Or maybe because that first chaste kiss was so satisfying.

For several long moments, their lips brushed and bumped together, sweet with cream and marshmallows. Then Zach threaded his fingers through Kristin's hair to cup her neck and nudge her just a little closer.

Kristin stroked his face, felt the faint prickle of his beard beneath her fingertips, smiled against his lips as he trailed his fingers down her neck to the slowly accelerating pulse at the base of her throat. She slid her hand from his jaw to the back of his collar and nudged him closer, too, prolonging the contact. Then she opened to his slick tongue.

It was inevitable. The slow, wet dance of their tongues quickly became a heated exchange, with hearts pounding and hands roughly exploring.

Zach broke from the kiss to shove the strawberries and cream aside, then in an apparent afterthought, pushed their picnic bags off the blanket and into the sand.

They fell to the blanket, mouths seeking, legs twining. Kristin's mind swam. His kisses were white-hot, insatiable, covering her cheeks, her mouth, her throat. He smelled of musk and salt air, and she inhaled deeply, drawing his scent straight into her belly. She felt his hand beneath her shirt, felt his fingers deftly do away with the front closure of her bra.

Then he was tugging her shirt over her head, and with a low groan, burrowing into her softness.

Chapter 10

Kristin's heart pounded as Zach's warm breath spilled over her breasts. *Oh, yes,* her heart sang. *Oh, yes.* She closed her eyes, loving the scrape of his beard on her skin. Loving him.

And she did love him—no matter how determined she'd been to ignore it, or how much she'd feared it. Maybe he didn't feel that way right now, but he'd been so vigilant, so warm, so tender toward her that it could become love if he would just let it in. If she'd had doubts about that before, his bailing out on a meeting he wanted and needed to attend erased every one of them.

Zach fumbled for her waistband and hooked his thick fingers inside to pull off her sweatpants. Then cotton and lace fell away, too, and Kristin was naked against him, thick plaid flannel soft against her back and legs.

"You're sure about this?" he rasped. "You know I care about you. But—"

"I know," she whispered, certain that he would come around eventually. For now, she would love enough for both of them.

Quickly, Zach undressed in the faint glow of the fire, light and shadow playing over his hard, lean torso. Kristin's heart hammered as he cast aside his shirt and unsnapped his jeans, stripped off his briefs and dropped to his knees.

A wisp of arousal curled through her as she took in his beautifully sculpted body, tanned where the sun hit, white where it didn't. Then she reached for him, and with a ragged sigh, Zach kissed her deeply and came to her.

Hair-roughened legs twined with soft, smooth ones until they found a perfect fit. Tongues plunged wetly. Then the ancient ritual began, bodies gliding and stroking each other until the heat in their hearts became a need in their souls.

Kristin's mind spun as Zach moved down to kiss her breasts, then inched lower, planting more kisses along her rib cage and belly. His hands were everywhere, magic, hinting at the pleasure to come. Teasing, readying, keying her nerve endings to fever pitch.

When he worked his way back up, he kissed her so deeply, she released a tattered gasp. "Zach, it's been thirteen years. I don't want to wait any longer."

He pulled half of the blanket over them. Then with one sleek thrust, they were one again.

The first tingle swept her away, shocking her with its swiftness and intensity. The second sent a dozen shivery sensations quaking through her. She wanted to wait, make it last. But there was no delaying those quickly building responses. Just before her breathing shut down and wave after wave washed through her, Kristin pressed her forehead to his throat and clung to him for dear life.

She'd scarcely caught her breath when Zach groaned and found his own shuddering release.

Long moments later, they lay blissfully sated, feeling their popping nerve ends ease and the beating of their hearts taper to some semblance of normalcy. Waves still crashed on the shore, and above, the moon still shone as if nothing profound had just happened. But it had.

Zach rolled onto his back, then brought Kristin flush against his side. She smiled, pillowing her head on his shoulder. He didn't have to hold her so close, she thought, though she loved the hard, muscular strength of him. She wasn't going anywhere. This was where she wanted to be for the rest of her life.

"Nice," he murmured in a gravely voice.

"Very," she agreed. Her fingers slid lazily through his chest hair and skimmed a nipple. She moved lower, to his flat, taut stomach and felt him shudder.

Laughter rustled deep in his throat. "Would it be tacky to say I've missed you this way?"

"Terribly," she murmured. "But I'll forgive you if you say you've missed me in other ways, too."

Zach lifted himself on an elbow. His smile in the fading glow of the fire filled her so completely, she never wanted the night to end.

"I have missed you in other ways. Remember when we used to talk about the company I'd have one day? Even at eighteen, you always said the right things. You made me believe in myself."

"Supporting you was my job back then," she returned with a smile. "And now, all of your hopes and dreams have come true."

Zach shook his head. "No, not all. But I'm working on the rest."

Kristin's heart leapt hopefully. Did he mean the two of them? Once he'd yearned for more than a company that would provide him with an income, stature and respect. He'd wanted her, too, and children he could love and nurture as his father had never nurtured him. But she couldn't ask him to explain himself. This closeness between them was too new, too fragile.

She stroked the hair at his temple, traced the curve of his ear. "I'm not sure what else you're looking for...but I suspect with your drive, you'll have it all one of these days."

"Think so?"

"Know so."

Zach's gaze drifted to her mouth again, and slowly, he brought his head down for another kiss. His low voice rumbled warmly. "How about that?" he said. "You still say all the right things."

A shrill sound that didn't belong there startled them both.

Quickly, Zach yanked their kicked-aside blanket back over them and froze in a semi-upright position. Then he shook his head and chuckled softly as his cell phone continued to ring somewhere in their pile of clothing.

He groped through the tangle of cotton and denim and shook it out of his shirt pocket.

Kristin stared numbly as he flipped it open on the third ring. He'd brought his phone down here with them?

"Davis. Yeah, Dan, how did it go?"

The words were barely out of his mouth when he seemed to switch gears and he looked back at Kristin. For a long moment, he stared at her in the dwindling light of the fire, his gaze flickering through a series of unreadable thoughts. Then without so much as a smile or a "just give me a minute," he turned back to his conversation and...*and shut her out?*

What was that look all about? What had happened in those few short moments to put distance between them? Why hadn't he continued to hold her while he'd talked? And why hadn't he told Dan that he'd call him back later? She listened, continuing to measure him in uneasy confusion.

"That's great. How soon do we need to start?" He paused. "No, the first team's promised to Mrs. Hart. We'll put the other crew on it. They should finish up at the mall in a few weeks."

Kristin pushed away her concerns. Everything was fine. He just needed to take the call, then they'd snuggle in their blanket again...talk about where they would go from here.

But as he became more deeply entrenched in his conversation and the ocean breezes grew cool, she had the sinking feeling that that wasn't going to happen. Something *was* wrong.

Kristin reached for her clothes.

He didn't even realize that she'd dressed until she touched his shoulder and pointed toward the beach house. The fire's embers and moonlight on white sand shed enough light to see his shadowy expression. Her heart began to pound. It was all business.

"Hang on a second, Dan," he said, cupping his hand over the phone. "You're going to the house?"

She forced a smile, hoping he'd return it. "I just

realized I have sand in places where sand shouldn't be. I need a shower.''

Reluctance, regret—something she couldn't place—touched his voice, but there was no smile. "Okay. I'll see you when I'm through here."

Tears stung her eyes. "Sure. I'll take some of our gear with me."

When he nodded and brought the phone to his ear again, the only clear thought in Kristin's mind was of Stephanie Michaels. *Don't fall for him,* she'd said. *You'll end up wondering what you did to scare him off.*

Suddenly she couldn't get away from him fast enough.

Zach watched her leave, then sighed raggedly and spoke into the phone again. "Dan, let's finish tomorrow at the trailer. It'll be easier with all the prints and specs in front of us."

"Okay." Dan paused, humor entering his voice. "Did you get your other business taken care of?"

"What other business?"

He was laughing softly now. "Well, considerin' what I walked in on this afternoon, and the way you tore out of the meetin' tonight, I figured it was woman business. Pete and Joe couldn't get over it. Kept sayin' it wasn't like you to skip out like that. They wondered if you were sick."

"I'll see you tomorrow," Zach grumbled, stopping the conversation before it had a chance to start. "At 6:00 a.m."

"Didn't go too good, huh?"

"Six," Zach repeated tersely, then snapped the phone shut. So his men were talking already. Great.

Scowling, he shook the sand out of his underwear and jeans and pulled them on, his mind already pondering new problems.

Okay, she was upset, and she had every reason to be. What he'd done was unforgivable. Dammit, he hadn't wanted to hurt her. But the second he'd heard Dan's voice, reality had smacked him right between the eyes.

He picked up his gritty sneakers and yanked them on without socks. For days, she'd owned his mind, and all he could think about was making love to her—in the bedroom, in the bathroom, in the kitchen, on the damn deck! And it was obvious that the attraction was mutual. Now they'd given in to it, and he was in trouble.

Zach snatched up the blanket and rolled it into a ball. He cared about her, but there could be nothing beyond that. It was too soon for a commitment to any woman, even Kris—assuming that she'd forgiven him and wanted a commitment, too. Minds got fuzzy when sex was involved.

His time was earmarked for building the biggest and best company he could put together. Davis Construction was his first priority. Because if he wasn't a success in business, he—

Zach froze, then stood staring out at the jet-black waters of the Atlantic and the sudsy white caps rolling to shore.

If he wasn't a success in business, he wasn't a success as a man.

That thought hit him hard. Unbidden, the images that had spawned that unintentional philosophy swam through his mind. Images of his drunken father...images of the mother who couldn't hack their

life and abandoned him. He thought of the years before Etta without decent food, without decent clothing,
without love...and swore again that he'd never put
anyone he cared for through that. It might take a while,
but he'd have plenty of security before he went to any
woman and asked her to stay. He'd deluded himself
before when he thought love was enough. It wasn't.
He and Kristin had been too young to realize that then.
Or maybe she *had* known.

Maybe that's why she'd shied away.

When he returned to the beach house almost twenty
minutes later, Kristin was in her room, and shower
mist hung in the bathroom and hall. Zach looked for
a strip of light beneath her closed door, saw none, and
knocked anyway. He knew she wasn't asleep.

Her stiff voice was muffled behind the door.
"What?"

"I just wanted to say good-night."

"Good night."

"Can I come in for a second?"

"It's your house."

Zach sighed. He had that coming. A wedge of light
from the hall spilled inside as he opened the door. She
was propped against the pillows, knees up, wet hair
slicked to her head, and the sheet primly covering her
nightshirt from the waist down. The scents of soap and
peaches were alive inside her room.

"What time do you need to head to the airport?"
he asked, relieved that she was leaving. He'd never
meant to hurt her, but withdrawing was the only way
he knew to deal with this.

"I've already made arrangements to be picked up."

"I can drive you. See you off."

"Don't. You obviously have things to do."

Zach felt a guilty tightening in his chest as he took in the determined set of her jaw. "All right," he replied, silently admitting his cowardice and knowing this would be easier. "Have a safe flight tomorrow."

"And you have a delightful day at work."

"Kris…"

"I've said all I'm going to say. My life is back in Wisdom. Yours is here."

Zach nodded, then closed the door and crossed the hall to his own room. He'd been thinking almost the same thing down on the beach, and they were both right. So why did her saying it aloud make him feel so hollow inside?

Kristin slid down on her pillow as the door closed, her emotions a mess of hurt and anger and frustration. But she would not cry. He wasn't worth her tears.

She understood that his business was a big part of his life, but at this hour, no information was so important that it couldn't have waited for ten minutes.

Just a few more whispers in the dark. Just a few more minutes in his arms—that's all she'd wanted. But Zach hadn't wanted that. He'd wanted to distance himself from her, and he'd done it beautifully.

She drew in a deep breath. Whatever level their relationship had mutated to for those few wonderful hours was gone now. How stupid she'd been to trust him with her heart again. Their lovemaking on the beach had only been sex to him. Sex and a few warm memories. She needed to go home.

The Wisdom Food Mart was bustling with customers two days later as Kristin walked up and down the aisles, throwing items into her cart. She had no idea

what she actually needed; she'd lost her list somewhere en route to the store. Her distraction was hardly
a surprise. She was still trying to recover from her ill-
advised trip to the beach, and her mind churned with
the disturbing news she'd received this morning.

She was nearing the brightly lit dairy case when her
nerve endings went on full alert. Zach was sidestep-
ping two elderly women and their shopping carts and
coming toward her. She almost turned away, but he'd
seen her, and she was obliged to hold her ground.

"Small world," he said, as though their parting had
been amiable.

"Is it?" she asked, not bothering to temper the chill
in her voice.

"Actually, yes." He unfolded the sheet of paper he
took from the pocket of his jeans and held up her
shopping list. "But as you can see, I didn't bump into
you by accident."

She blinked, startled. "Where did you find that?"

"Beside the door to your apartment. I figured you
still shopped here, not at one of the big chains outside
of town, so this was my first stop. I saw your van in
the parking lot."

"Then I guess you get an A in detective work."

Ignoring her sarcasm, he handed her the list. "How
are you?"

"Oh, I'm just great," she answered, needing to lash
out at someone. Or maybe she just needed to lash out
at him. "I found out this morning that the fire was
arson."

Zach's expression sobered. "What's being done?"

Averting her gaze, she reached for a six-pack of
yogurt and dropped it in her cart. She wasn't in the
mood for forgiveness, and that caring look in his gray

eyes always got to her. "Chad's handling the investigation," she replied, pushing forward again. "He asked me for a list of possible suspects. He even questioned Will Arnett while I was with y—while I was gone."

Zach set a half gallon of milk in her cart. "The Arnetts are in town? I thought they left days ago."

Kristin kept walking. "Will Arnett came back alone. He claimed his mother wanted a few more items from Anna Mae's house before the auction."

"Claimed?" Zach asked.

"He's lying."

"How do you know?"

"Because the day after the fire, Mrs. Arnett told me she thought Anna Mae's ghost was responsible for the blaze. She's into psychic readings, and she has this strange notion that Anna Mae wants her home kept intact. Besides, the way Mildred and her son fought when they were here together, I can't imagine her sending him back for anything. She doesn't trust him."

He grabbed her cart, stopping her progress. "Hard to regain trust when it's broken, isn't it?"

Kristin stared pointedly at him. *Yes, it was, and he'd just done it again at the beach.* She picked up his milk and jammed it into his hands. "I'm not paying for this."

"I didn't ask you to." Zach dodged her cart as she swung around him and moved toward the bread display. "So Chad wants a list of potential suspects?"

"I can't give him one." She sent him another sharp look. "Most people I know wouldn't hurt me."

A nerve worked in his jaw. "I can't imagine anyone

wanting to hurt you. But sometimes people don't think things through before they act."

"Really?" She threw English muffins into the cart and kept going. She knew they were talking about his imbecilic behavior at the beach, but it wasn't an apology, and she wasn't going to tell him everything was fine. Staring straight ahead, she headed for the checkout clerk with the shortest line.

He was beside her again. "Maybe if we put our heads together we can come up with someone."

"Someone who's thoughtless and inconsiderate?"

He released an irritated blast of air. "No, someone who might have wanted to burn your shop to the ground."

"You and I will come up with this list?"

"We could try."

"Where?"

"Wherever you want."

Kristin turned to him and lowered her voice so the surrounding customers wouldn't hear. "Is this just a way to get me into bed again? Why are you really here?"

For a long moment, Zach's gaze fused with hers. Then he said in a quietly controlled voice that indicated he'd had enough, "You know what? Suddenly, I don't have a goddamn clue."

Without another word, he squeezed past two women already unloading their purchases and handed the milk to the overweight teenage boy bagging groceries. Zach dug two bills from his jeans and slapped them into the boy's hand. The kid lit up like a Christmas tree.

"I've changed my mind about the milk. Can you return it for me?"

"I sure can!" the boy said. "Thanks!"

"No, thank *you*."

An instant later, he was striding toward the automatic doors and was gone.

Chapter 11

Three hours later, Kristin turned into Etta Gardner's driveway and drove up to the big, clapboard farmhouse. There was no sign of Zach, but the front porch looked good with new support posts and floorboards, and several new steps. The first thing she noticed when she got out of the van was the sound of a power saw somewhere behind the house. The second thing was the smell of freshly cut lumber.

Kristin took two plastic grocery bags from the van, slammed the door, then squared her shoulders and marched back toward those sounds and smells. She stopped short when she saw him, then raised her chin and kept walking. Wearing nothing but frayed, cut-off denim shorts and sneakers, Zach was just turning off a table saw.

His gaze collided with hers, and instantly turned dark as thunderheads. She didn't care. She wasn't here to make friends.

Scooping up a stack of boards, he crossed the short space of grass to the back porch. He laid the planks in the empty spaces between the old, gray ones, then grabbed the power drill beside him.

"I can hold them down so they don't shift while you're drilling," she offered coolly. "If you want me to."

Zach looked up, his gaze barely tolerant. "Suit yourself."

Kristin set her bags down, then stepped over a maze of electric cords and ascended to the porch. She'd known this meeting wouldn't be a walk in the park, but there was something pressing on her mind, and he was the only person she could use as a sounding board.

And with all of that, as she crouched beside him, steadying the boards while he drilled holes then filled them with long deck screws, she was unable to pull her gaze from him.

Sawdust clung to the frizz of hair on his chest and stuck to his arms. Sweat trickled from his temples. Zach wiped it away, replaced the last board, then laid the drill and power screwdriver aside and straightened. Even the black hair falling over his forehead couldn't soften the uncompromising lines on his face.

"My turn to ask," he said, his frosty gaze meeting hers. "Why are *you* really here? Hoping to get me into bed?"

"I brought your milk over," she said crisply. "You obviously wanted it, or you wouldn't have picked it up."

"So you paid for it and drove it all the way out here." It was a statement, not a question.

"Yes."

Zach's turbulent gaze ran from her short-sleeved white blouse and black watchplaid shorts to her legs and sandals. Then he reached into the cooler near the steps and grabbed two cans of ginger ale. He offered her one, and she took it. "Is that the only reason you came by?"

"No." If he was waiting for an apology, he'd be waiting a long time. "Among other things, I thought we should talk about what happened at the beach."

"The beach."

"Yes."

He drank deeply, then wiped his mouth with his forearm. "Which part?"

"The crappy part. I came by to tell you that you didn't have to brush me off after we'd..." She wouldn't call it lovemaking because he obviously hadn't viewed it that way. "...after we'd been together. I heard you loud and clear when you said you weren't looking for anything beyond the moment, and that was fine with me. As the old saw goes, man doesn't live by bread alone. Neither does woman."

Those last words seemed to startle him—maybe even annoy him—and a second after his gaze sharpened, he started unplugging cords and returning tools to the large chest by the back door. He still sounded edgy a minute later when he asked, "Heard anything new on the fire?"

"No. But I've been out most of the day." She settled stiffly on the top porch step. When he'd finished putting his tools away, he sat, too, a polite distance away. Kristin snapped the tab on her soft drink. "Aren't you going to ask about the other things I wanted to discuss?"

"All right. I'm asking."

"I want to call a cease-fire for a while."

"Any particular reason?"

"Yes, I...I need your opinion on something."

That brought a look of surprise. There was even more surprise when she told him what it was, but it was fleeting and he quickly erased everything but cool detachment from his face.

"I read Anna Mae's most recent journal from start to finish last night. I don't think her death was an accident."

"According to Chad, blood and hair on the corner of the coffee table proved that a blow to the head was the cause of death," he answered. "I'd guess that killing someone with a piece of furniture would require some pretty fancy choreography."

Kristin tamped down her irritation. "I'm not saying that anyone choreographed anything. I'm saying that I think someone helped her fall. And if the fall hadn't produced the desired result, maybe that someone would've finished the job using more conventional means."

Zach tipped back his head and finished his ginger ale, his long throat working greedily and captivating Kristin despite the mood he'd put her in. She reached down beside her and lifted both bags to the porch, one containing his milk, the other the journal she'd mentioned. She opened it to the page she wanted him to read.

Zach met her eyes for a moment, then set his empty can down and pulled the journal onto his lap. He read aloud.

"This is dreadfully difficult because I once cared for him. But though I have overlooked his small transgressions, I cannot sit idly by and ignore this one. I have evidence of his crime safely hidden, and I know I must tell him and insist that he turn himself in. I believe the authorities would be much more lenient on him. But I truly fear a confrontation, particularly since I don't have irrefutable proof. He hides a vicious temper.''

Zach met her eyes again. "She can't be talking about Harlan Greene. Frankly, I can't see Harlan doing anything wrong."

"I can't either, but I really don't know him all that well. What if he *did* do something to Anna Mae? What if she told him what she knew, and he got so angry that he shoved her into that table?"

"Again, what could Harlan have done that was so bad? The guy's damn near eighty."

"He's seventy-five. He's also a tax collector who gambles."

Zach drew the same conclusion she had. "Embezzlement?"

"It's the only thing I could think of. I scoured the book looking for hints that it might be Harlan, but in the later journals, Anna Mae was vague about people's identities. I only recognized my mother in her writings because she described the gifts she left on our porch."

"Did you find out what her evidence was?"

"Photographs. But I don't know where she hid them. That makes me think that this man knew she kept journals. Maybe she was afraid he'd read them and find the photos on his own."

Zach handed the book back to her. "Pretty thin. Have you shown this to Hollister?"

"Not yet. I wanted to talk it through with you first. Regardless of anything else I might be feeling, I value your opinion."

Again, there was a flicker of something in his eyes, but his face remained impassive. Kristin set her soft drink aside and took a deep breath because there was more to tell. "Zach, I think that Anna Mae's death, the man in her attic and the fire at my shop are all connected."

This time he reacted. His dry, skeptical look wasn't what she wanted to see.

Kristin stood and headed for her van. "Never mind. If you're going to act like I'm a twelve-year-old playing Nancy Drew, I'll see Chad right now." Her voice dropped to a mutter. "I just keep making mistake after mistake with you."

"Wait."

"No." She felt him behind her, and she turned to face him as she latched onto the van's door handle. "I just thought that you might give a damn since you seemed so grateful to Anna Mae for helping you once."

"I do give a damn. But obviously, I haven't given this as much thought as you have. Tell me why you think all three events are connected, and I'll try to keep an open mind. I wasn't in a very receptive mood when you got here."

"You're still not in a very receptive mood."

"Potshots? I thought we'd declared a cease-fire."

Kristin stilled. He was right.

"Do you want to tell me the rest of it?" Zach prompted.

"Yes." She needed to get things straight in her head before she saw Chad.

"Do you mind if we talk by the pond? I'd like to rinse some of this sawdust off."

"Fine."

But beneath her squared shoulders and cool reply, she did mind. There were memories all around her, the most poignant in the whitewashed barn where they'd first made love, the most hurtful in the tall weeds behind it that led to the Wilder farm. But Gretchen was gone now, and she had to put those memories away, once and for all. Holding onto them served no useful purpose.

Zach motioned her to an old wooden bench a few feet from the water's edge, and Kristin complied, her sandals all but disappearing in the fine, calf-high grass.

She sat stiffly as he bent to splash his face, arms and chest, trying to ignore the play of sunlight on his tanned back. Then he was beside her, combing his wet hair back with both hands.

"Okay. Why do you think all three events are related?" Water beaded on his skin, a few rivulets sliding down his taut midsection and pooling in the whorl of hair at his navel.

She glanced away. "Some of this is going to sound far-fetched."

"Go on."

"All right. If the man in the journals knew Anna Mae had photos linking him to a crime, he might have been searching for them in the attic the night I was there. I'm assuming that he's already searched the rest of the house. He would've had ample opportunity because it was empty for weeks while Anna Mae's will was being probated. Besides, if he got inside the night I discovered him, he certainly could have gained entry before that." She met Zach's grave expression. "Still with me?"

"Still with you," he said, but it didn't appear to please him.

"Okay. While I was tagging the items I wanted that night, I noticed that someone had made a mess of Anna Mae's bedroom. They hadn't trashed it, but a few of the photographs and pictures on the walls were tipped, and clothing stuck out of one of the dresser drawers. I thought the Arnetts had done it. Now..."

"Now you're not sure."

"Yes. That brings us to the fire at my shop. What if the intruder didn't find the photos that night? Wouldn't he wonder if they were hidden inside one of the pieces I'd bought? To make sure they never saw the light of day he could have—"

"—torched your shop."

Kristin nodded.

Zach frowned at a clump of dandelions at his feet. "Okay. I don't know a thing about criminal investigations, but I have to say that this theory of yours assumes a lot of things. Who knew you'd bought the contents of Anna Mae's attic?"

"You, me, the Arnetts, Eli, Harlan..." She rolled her eyes. "The all-seeing, all-knowing Elyssa Spectral. A lot of people knew—customers who came into my shop, passersby the day of the delivery. This man could have easily heard about it. He could've even been watching Anna Mae's house."

Zach plucked off a few dandelion heads and tossed them, one by one onto the surface of the pond. "For the sake of argument, let's assume that everything you've said is right on the money. Why didn't the arsonist torch Anna Mae's house, too?"

Kristin sighed. This was why she'd wanted to discuss her suspicions with him first. "I thought of that, too. The only thing I could come up with was, maybe this guy was sure the photos weren't *in* the house.

Chad and his men searched it twice, first during their investigation into Anna Mae's death, then after I was pushed down the stairs.''

"But they wouldn't have searched it in the same way."

"That's true. But I'm betting that the intruder did an exhaustive search. Then there's another possibility. If Will Arnett—not Harlan—was the arsonist, he wouldn't have burned down a home he stood to make money on.''

"I thought his mother inherited everything.''

"She did. But even though they bicker constantly, Will is probably her heir. Mildred's a widow, and he's her only child.'' Kristin faced him again. "So? What do you think?''

Zach's gray gaze settled on hers, and the attraction she'd been fighting quaked through her again.

"I think it's *possible*.'' But his expression said that there was still a lot of room for doubt.

Suddenly, something that should have occurred to her long before this hit Kristin. Energized, she pushed to her feet and started walking toward the driveway. "Thank you for listening. I have to go.''

Zach leapt to his feet, too, her sudden departure toppling his rigid demeanor. "Where?''

"To the lake. Not all of Anna Mae's things were delivered that day. The rest are at Lakeside storage. Those snapshots could be hidden inside something that never made it to my shop.''

"Wait a minute!'' Zach came after her, obviously annoyed.

"No. I need to do this right now.''

"Why?''

"Because…'' She faced him, tired of being stiff and

cool when she felt so passionate about all of it. "Because I got to know Anna Mae when I was reading her journals, and I *liked* her, Zach. She was gentle and kind and went to great lengths to help anyone who needed it. She helped my mother. She helped you. She put up with dysentery and fevers and unsanitary conditions to help men and women she'd never met. If her death wasn't an accident, I want to know who took her life. She cared about everyone—even the criminal she wrote about. It's time someone cared about *her*."

Zach studied the determination on her face for another long moment, then sighed. He didn't completely buy the scenario she'd laid out, but if the arsonist and the intruder who'd pushed her *were* the same person...and that man knew that some of Anna Mae's things were in Kristin's storage bay...he might still be nervous about those snapshots. Then there was the debt that he, too, owed Anna Mae. She *had* been a wonderful woman.

"Give me a minute to put some clothes on," he growled. "I'm going with you."

"Why?"

"Because now you've got me imagining weird things, too, and I think someone should be with you in case your bogeyman shows up."

"He can't possibly know about my storage unit."

"You're probably right."

"Then why do you want to go with me?"

Zach hesitated, not sure he wanted to examine that question too closely. "Would you rather I didn't?"

"No. I could use some help going through the boxes."

"Then I'll be right out."

Zach went inside and pulled on a shirt from the

folded pile on the chair, then shoved his wallet into
the back pocket of his cut-offs. She'd been a pain in
the neck this morning, but she'd already toppled down
a flight of stairs and someone had torched her building.
There was nothing wrong with a little caution and a
healthy respect for the unknown. That didn't mean he
wanted to drape her in diamonds and throw flowers at
her feet. It only meant he didn't want her to get hurt.

"Ready?" he asked, coming back out.

She nodded. "We'll take my van and stop at the
station to see Chad first."

Zach sent her a deadpan look. "Oh, good."

But Hollister was out when they reached the station,
so Kristin jotted a short note of explanation and left
the journal with Patrolman Larry McIntyre.

Now, as Zach got out of Kristin's van and looked
out over the marina, he watched white gulls squawk
and wheel above Lake Edward's greenish-blue waters.
He was reminded of home, but there was no sand here,
no breakers crashing, no houses on stilts. Everything
around him was lush and green, trees, underbrush and
grass marching all the way to the muddy shoreline.

He fell into step beside her as Kristin crossed the
gravel lot beside Lakeside Self-Storage and headed for
the last unit on the right. She bent low to unlock the
door, then Zach pushed it up, garage-door style.

Shrieks and revving motors yanked their attention
back to the marina, and they watched through the trees
as someone on a Jet Ski flew across the water. Edward
wasn't as large as some other lakes, but it obviously
had enough size to satisfy everyone's needs. There
was even a stately white riverboat with a huge paddle
wheel moored near the slips holding smaller craft.

"Is that the riverboat they booked for the bachelor cruise?" he asked.

Kristin's eyes clouded for a second, then she nodded and entered the bay.

It was smaller than he had expected. Or maybe it just looked that way because the center aisle was so narrow. Cartons lined both sides, and against the far wall, several large items were draped in mud-green quilts.

Zach pulled off the heavy covers and tossed them on a stack of boxes. There were chairs, an old curio cabinet, a rolltop desk, and a treadle sewing machine with a fancy wrought-iron foot pedal. A huge, bamboo birdcage sat atop two steamer trunks stacked in a corner, and a set of gaudy, black dog lamps with tasseled red shades stood on the floor beside them.

Kristin moved to his side. Her perfume in the confined area did strange things to his system. "Where do you want to start?" he asked, determined to keep this platonic. Determined to keep it the way she wanted it.

"I don't care as long as we don't miss anything."

He set the birdcage aside and picked up one of the trunks. "Then let's start with these."

Zach carried the first one to the center of the room where the light was better, then returned for the second.

He glanced at her again as she lifted the birdcage to inspect the bottom. The interest in her eyes reminded him that the pieces here weren't just hiding places for secrets. They were acquisitions for the new shop she hoped to build.

He cleared his throat. "I found those floor plans you

sketched when you were at my place. Have you seen an architect yet?"

"Not yet," she answered indifferently. "I want to see a check from the insurance company first. Actually," she went on, "a man I used to date has already offered his help. I'm seeing him next Monday. He just opened an office in Lancaster."

Adrenaline fused Zach to the spot. A man in Lancaster? An ex-lover? He stared at her for a long moment, then told himself he didn't care and crouched to open the first trunk. He lifted out a chest that looked like a big mahogany jewelry box.

Raising the hinged lid, he saw that it was empty, then checked the double row of thin, side-by-side drawers and set it aside. He glanced at her again before he unpacked the rest—old puzzles, a few board games and a thick bundle of greeting cards, tied with binding twine.

Apparently satisfied that the birdcage held no secrets, Kristin joined him, quickly taking charge. She handed him the stack of cards. "If you'll search through these, I'll check the games. Okay?"

"Sure." But he wasn't thinking about incriminating photographs right now, dammit. He was still thinking about an architect in Lancaster who'd heard about the fire at Kristin's shop and phoned to offer his services.

Long, bare legs drew his attention as she fanned through Monopoly money. And something primitive thudded in his blood as he remembered how soft they'd felt under his hands...how silky smooth her thighs were, all the way up to where her faint tan ended and the curve of her bottom began.

The Monopoly box hit the floor with a thwack, and

she picked up another game. Then she seemed to sense him staring at her and looked up. "What?"

"Nothing."

"It doesn't look like nothing." Spotting the still-bundled cards in his hands, she sighed wearily. "All right, you think this is a waste of time when you have work to do back at Etta's. Or you're still annoyed about this morning. Whatever. If you want, I'll take you back to the farm."

"That's not it."

"Then why are you staring at me?"

Zach shrugged and untied the cards, but underneath, his gut was knotted and his libido was hearing the call of the wild. "You just look pretty today." He grumbled to dilute the compliment he'd been forced to give, but didn't raise his head to gauge her reaction. "I must be getting used to your hair."

Crickets were chirping below a rising moon when they finally sat back on those furniture covers and gave up. Some time ago, their crouched legs had begun to cramp. Zach had folded the dusty throws into a padded seat and turned on the overhead light.

"You're disappointed," he said.

She nodded. "I really thought we'd find those snapshots. For Anna Mae. And even for me. While we were searching, I couldn't help thinking that if we found them, and the same man was linked to the fire at my shop, the insurance company would stop dragging their feet."

"It's only been eight days. Just be glad you had blanket coverage instead of a policy that requires you to list every item and its worth. It would be months before the appraisers decided what you had coming."

"I know. I don't mean to whine. I just need to get my life back. I need—"

She needed everything. She needed for all of this to be resolved. She needed money to rebuild. And despite the fact that she and Zach had an unspoken pact, despite the fact that it would be a large mistake, she needed to be held. They'd made love. They'd been as intimate as two people could be. Now, though they'd spoken easily while they'd searched, the distance between them felt foreign and cold. Felt wrong.

Standing, she brushed off the seat of her shorts. "Let's go. I want to stop by the office and see if Chad's had a chance to look at the journal." She released a short, mirthless laugh. "He probably thinks I'm crazy, too."

Zach carried the quilts over to drape the furniture again. "I don't think you're crazy. And I'd bet my eye teeth that Hollister won't accuse you of that, either."

"Why not? You said yourself that my theory assumed too much. I believe 'thin' was the word you used."

He walked back to her. "Why not? Because a man who wants something doesn't say things that will screw it up. And it's pretty obvious he wants you."

She knew that. But it would probably never happen. Even though it was the worst thing in the world for her, she wanted someone else. Kristin moved to the light switch beside the galvanized door and waited for him to exit. Then she clicked off the switch, and let Zach pull down the door and secure the padlock.

As she walked to her van, she glanced at the gritty stones underfoot, glanced up at the moths fluttering in the wash of the light poles…glanced at the trees, dark blots against the night sky.

She glanced anywhere but at him.

Chapter 12

Kristin watched as Zach entered the farmhouse, turned on a light, then closed the door behind him. Blinking rapidly, she backed out of the dark driveway.

"Be careful going home," he'd warned. *"Looks like the fog's rolling in."*

"I will. Thanks for your help."

"Sure. Good night."

And that was that. There'd been no kiss, no touch, no "See you soon." Just a polite, civilized parting that echoed how the entire day had gone. She knew it was for the best, but she couldn't shake that hollow, empty feeling.

Overhead, a sliver of moon bobbed in and out of the clouds, now and then shedding a little light on a landscape of tall grasses and sturdy fence posts. But for the most part, the only things penetrating the thickening fog and darkness were the van's headlights.

Kristin's throat tightened as she drove past intersecting roads and bumped through a washboard of ruts.

Why did she still want him so much? Why didn't those deep down feelings of mistrust and his insane workaholic lifestyle turn her away from him? Why didn't it send her running in the opposite direction? That's how a smart woman would react. That's how Rachel would react. But then, Rachel was the sensible sister. Or rather, she'd become sensible after she'd followed the man she loved to Arizona, only to have him cheat on her and marry someone else. Now caution was her middle name.

Headlights came out of nowhere, spearing her eyes in the rearview mirror.

Kristin's heart vaulted into her throat. *What was going on? What was happening?* The vehicle raced toward her, closing the distance between them far too fast for coincidence.

Mind spinning wildly, she floored the gas pedal. The car hugging her bumper had to have been lying in wait—parked with his lights off on one of the side roads she'd passed. This road dead-ended in a field at the edge of Etta's property!

Kristin flew over the road, dust billowing behind her as she slashed quick looks into the mirror—tried to identify the vehicle. The headlights nearly blinded her again. Gripping the steering wheel, she careened around a curve in the road and drove through another series of shuddering ruts.

Daring to take her right hand from the wheel, she unlatched the storage compartment between the bucket seats and fumbled for her cell phone. But as she yanked it out, shaky fingers lost their hold, and the phone bounced to the floor on the passenger's side.

Kristin's heart sank and her lungs threatened to shut down. She grabbed the wheel with both hands again.

Chad's warnings clanged in her mind as trees whizzed by her side windows.

Dammit, Kristin, didn't you think I'd worry if you disappeared after your shop was burned? Especially when arson was suspected?

Was the man who'd pushed her, the man who'd burned her shop now trying to run her off the road?

Make a list of possible suspects—anyone you think might have a grudge against you.

A halo of light appeared in the distant fog, and Kristin's pulse leapt. The road was ending. The mall was just ahead. *People and safety* were just ahead.

A stop sign appeared. Kristin sped through it, hanging a left and fishtailing onto the paved road to race toward the ever-brightening lights ahead. Her stomach lurched as she glanced in the mirror and saw headlights again.

"Come on, come on," she begged, willing the van to go faster. Finally, she was at the entrance to the mall, spiking her brake and swerving into the lot. She let out a dismayed breath. A flashy red truck with an extended cab was the only vehicle there.

Kristin hit the gas pedal again and roared toward the two young couples standing beside the truck, praying that there truly was safety in numbers. Turning the wheel hard, she squealed to a stop a few yards from the gaping teenagers, then turned, wide-eyed, to stare at the driver who'd just sailed in beside her.

A rage she'd never felt before rose in her. Kristin unhooked her seat belt and bolted from the van. The man driving the white Blazer did the same. He looked every bit as agitated as she was.

"Have you lost your mind?" Chad shouted, coming around the front of the SUV to meet her. He was dressed in jeans and a sport shirt, not his uniform, and he was furious.

"Have you lost *yours?*" she fired back. "What were you thinking, chasing me like that? We could've both been killed!"

"I wasn't chasing you, I was trying to signal you to pull over! Didn't you see me flicking my beams on and off?"

"No! I was too busy trying to keep my van on the road. What were you doing out there?"

Instead of answering, Chad turned to scowl at the teenagers clustered near the truck, their attention riveted on the argument. "Okay, break it up," he demanded in a voice full of authority. "We have a loitering ordinance in this town. If you don't move right now, I'll call a patrol car and *have* you moved."

The two pretty brunettes obeyed and climbed into the back seat. The boys played it a little cooler, laughing and joking under their breaths as they took their time getting into the front and fastening their seat belts. Finally, the driver gunned the engine and slowly drove off, laughter rolling through the open windows. Kristin could feel Chad's temper sear the air around them.

"I was looking for you," he said coldly, turning back to her and returning to her original question. "*That's* what I was doing out there. I went to your place after I read the note you stuck in the journal. I wanted to talk to you about it. But you weren't there."

"So you decided to see if I was at Zach's? You decided to spy on me?"

"No! I decided to track you down. There's a big difference."

"You were waiting for me with your lights out on a secluded dirt road. If that's not spying, I don't know what is."

Chad took her by the shoulders, his voice dropping low and shaky as his anger melted away. "Kristin, I love you."

She tried to pull away. "Don't say that."

"I have to. I love you, and I was afraid you might be right about this unnamed man looking for Anna Mae's photographs. I needed to find you."

"Let go of me."

Chad stared at her for a time, his face lining in the saffron glow of the lampposts. Then, slowly, he released her along with a burdened breath. "When there was no one at Davis's place, but his truck was there, I figured you were with him and you'd come back eventually. So, I waited."

"But you didn't wait in the driveway, Chad. You waited in the dark, like a—" She couldn't say "stalker," but that's what she was thinking.

He finished her sentence, all the fight gone out of him. "I waited in the dark like a man who didn't want to look like a complete fool in front of another man." He touched her cheek, and though she wanted to withdraw, she didn't. They'd been friends for too many years.

"Kristin, what do you think is going to happen here?" he asked in a voice full of sincerity. "Do you think Davis is going to dump a thriving business in North Carolina and come back here to you? Do you think he's going to put a ring on your finger and pledge his undying love? Buy a station wagon and put up a picket fence?"

Chad searched her eyes. "Well, he's had thirteen years to do it, if that's what he wanted. And it hasn't happened yet, has it? He hasn't done any of those things."

She didn't want to hear any more. "Good night, Chad." Kristin opened the door to her van. He slammed it shut again.

Her anger flared.

"What brought him back here?" Chad asked, his patience and apologetic manner gone again. "His aunt. He came back here to help Etta Gardner sell her farm. He didn't come back to patch things up with his high school steady. Dammit, Kristin, wake up! Do you want to be just another pretty little convenience—"

"Stop it!"

"—until he goes back home? Gretchen Wilder's not available anymore. All you are to Davis is someone handy to nail when he gets horn—"

Kristin slapped his face so hard, Chad's head snapped back. The act was so quick, so instinctive, her mind barely had time to register her intent.

They were both stunned.

Seconds ticked into full moments as their shocked gazes held and Kristin's heart sank. Dear God…she'd never struck anyone in her life. Not ever. Physical violence was repugnant to her.

"I'm so sorry," she whispered.

Miserable, Chad shook his head. "Don't apologize. I had that coming. I—I said too much. And I shouldn't have compared you to her. Gretchen was nothing. You're…you're everything."

Regret for a friendship that was now impossible to

continue made her want to cry. He truly had said too much. "It's late. We should both be getting home."

Chad's gaze clung to hers for a long moment, then nodding, he opened the door for her. He waited until she was behind the wheel to speak again. "Let's talk tomorrow about the journal. I'm off until three. I could come by in the morning with coffee and donuts."

Kristin shook her head. "I don't think so. Why don't you call me later in the day and we'll set something up?"

"That sounds like an appointment," he replied quietly. "Not like two people who care about each other getting together." When she remained silent, he sighed. "You're not even going to make up a flimsy excuse, are you? We're just not having breakfast."

"Yes." It hurt to answer that way, but she couldn't handle this much adoration or jealousy. He needed to look elsewhere for his happiness. If it took backing away to make him realize that, then that's what she had to do. She knew from experience that that kind of therapy worked. It was what Zach had done to her.

"All right," he said, squaring his shoulders and finding his pride again. "I'll phone you tomorrow, and we'll keep it to police business." He closed her door. The rest of his words were muffled, and probably not meant for her to hear. "I'll take whatever I can get."

Twenty minutes later, shivering and huddled deeply into her pile robe, Kristin stood over the range, waiting for water to heat. The outside temperature was still in the high sixties, but she couldn't get warm. Her teeth chattered and her nerve endings pulsed like live wires.

Post Traumatic Stress Syndrome?

No, probably nothing that exotic. But the night and

its fears had come rushing back like an unwelcome party guest the second she'd hurried inside her apartment and locked the door behind her.

It was only Chad, she kept telling herself. But if she was right about her shop fire and Anna Mae's death, it could've been someone else tailing her tonight. Someone dangerous.

The teakettle whistled shrilly. Kristin snatched it off the burner to silence it, then poured water over the chamomile leaves in the teapot she usually saved for special occasions. She needed to surround herself with pretty things tonight. Chad's jealousy and the sorrowful way he'd told her he loved her still had her insides quaking.

What was she going to do about him? He was her friend and devoted ally, a man who would give her the stars if it were in his power. But what he'd said and done tonight was—

The doorbell buzzed, followed by an insistent rapping at the door. *Now what?*

"Kris? Kris, open up!"

Zach? Kristin hurried into the small foyer off her living room to peer through the fisheye on her door. Startled and relieved to see him, she unlocked the door and pulled it open.

Before she could say a word, he was inside, shutting the door, and staring accusingly. "Don't you return calls? I left two messages on your answering machine asking you to phone me when you got in. Didn't you get them?"

"No, I—" Her voice caught. "The machine's in my room. I didn't notice the light blinking when I was in there." She'd been in too big a hurry to find something warm to wear. "What did you want?"

"I was worried about you driving home in the fog. I called to make sure you were okay." Suddenly he looked at her, really looked. He searched her face and eyes, dropped to her pile robe and the nervous hands pressing her collar to her throat.

"What's wrong?" he asked, his brow lining.

Kristin glanced away. "Nothing. I'm just cold."

"You're *cold?* It must be seventy degrees. Are you sick?"

"No."

"Then what's going on?"

She wished she knew. She was too sensible to be losing control like this. She went back to the kitchen and opened the cupboard. "Do you want a cup of tea? It's chamomile. Some people don't like it."

"I'd rather have an explanation. When you dropped me off you looked fine. Now you're as white as a sheet."

She reached for another china cup. In the next second, it seemed to fly out of her hand, smashing to the floor and scattering shards everywhere.

"Dammit, I can't hold onto anything tonight!" she cried. *"First my cell phone, now—"*

To her mortification, she began to cry.

Swearing quietly, Zach strode into the kitchen, lifted her in his arms, then carried her to the sofa in the living room. After checking her bare feet for glass, he sank down on the cushion beside her. His face was so close, she could see every line of concern and confusion on it.

"Kris, for the love of heaven, tell me what's going on. What did you mean about dropping your cell phone? Who were you going to call?"

She wiped her eyes and pulled herself together. "It doesn't matter."

"Dammit, Kris!"

"Nine-one-one! I was going to call for help!"

He looked stunned. "Why would you need—?"

"Because I was being chased. Or rather, I thought I was being chased."

"By whom? Who did you think it was? Did you get a look at him? Kris?"

Thoroughly stressed out now, she said, "Yes. I saw him, I got a look at him, and I know him. But if I tell you who it was, you have to promise not to do anything about it. I can't handle any more craziness tonight."

"Who?"

"Promise me."

"All right, I promise. Who was it?"

Kristin drew a deep breath, then let it out. "Chad."

His reaction was exactly what she expected. "*Chad* was following you?"

"He was waiting on one of the side roads near the farmhouse. He saw me take you home, and I don't think he liked it very much." When she told him the rest of it, his face turned to stone.

Zach shot to his feet. "Is he working tonight? Is he at the station? Or is he hiding out in the big house his parents left him?"

"Zach, let it go. He was jealous and upset. He didn't mean to scare me."

"He didn't mean to, but he sure as hell did, didn't he?"

He started for the door, but Kristin jumped up and grabbed his hand. "Don't. I'm all right. With everything that's happened lately, I just overreacted. I'm okay now." And it was the truth. Telling someone, getting it all out, had been cathartic. Or maybe she was calm now because Zach was here and she felt safe. As for Chad, he'd suffered enough. "Zach, you promised me—"

"That was before you told me what the son of a bitch did."

Then suddenly their history of broken trusts hung there between them. "You promised," she said distinctly. "Can I trust you to keep your word or not?"

Sighing, Zach nodded, his eyes still full of turmoil. Stepping closer, he smoothed his hands over the mint-green pile at her shoulders, then slid them under her thick collar to slowly massage her neck. It was all Kristin could to keep from easing into his hands.

"You've certainly had your share of trouble lately," he said, still disturbed.

"Better days are coming. Isn't that what people always say?"

"They also say 'an eye for an eye.' Chad's a bully and a hothead. He should've been arrested for what he did tonight."

She knew that. She also knew that talking about it anymore was pointless. It was done. It was over. She wanted to put it behind her. "Would you like that cup of tea now? Give me a minute to find my slippers and sweep up the mess I made, then I'll—"

"I'll do it. Where do you keep your broom and dustpan?"

"I can do it."

"No," he repeated succinctly. "*I'll* do it. Now, where do you keep them?"

The stubbornness in his eyes told her it was useless to argue. "All right, thank you. They're in the narrow cupboard beside the refrigerator.'' She shrugged out of her robe. ''I'll be right back.''

But as she prepared to leave, she realized that he was staring hard at her clothes. Heat crept into her cheeks. She hadn't changed to a nightgown when she'd returned. She'd been shivering so hard, she'd only taken the time to pull her robe over her shorts and blouse.

''I'm warm now,'' she said weakly.

''And I'm really sorry I made you that promise.''

When she returned dressed in lightweight gray sweats, he'd cleaned up the mess, and two cups were sitting on her small oak table. He waited for her to sit, then took the chair across from her.

''I've been thinking,'' he said. A nerve still worked in his jaw.

''About what?''

''About you. You need to have some fun. Maybe we both do.''

Kristin laughed shortly. ''Fun? What's that?''

''My point exactly.'' He tried to poke his thick fingers through the dainty china cup's handle, then scowling, gave up and held it by the bowl. ''I want to go on the cruise.''

''Sure you do,'' she replied dryly.

''I'm serious.''

''So am I.'' She knew how his mind worked. He was scrambling for a way to make things right; if he couldn't work his frustrations out on Chad, he'd try to do something nice for her. But that wasn't his job. ''You weren't interested in going before.''

''Now I am. When I saw the boat this afternoon, it occurred to me that it might be a good time. How about it?''

"No."

"Why not?"

For the same reason she shouldn't have gone to North Carolina with him. They had an understanding now, and she didn't want to confuse the issue. It was difficult enough to abide by it with him sitting so close to her. "Because I don't want to," she said. "And because you're just asking me out of pity."

"I don't make pity dates. Come on."

"I thought you wanted to finish Etta's house and get back home."

"I do, and I will. But all work and no play makes Zach a dull boy."

A shivery warmth moved through her as she took in his dark good looks and panther grace. There wasn't a dull bone in his long, lean body. Still, she shook her head. "You're only asking me to go because I was upset."

"No, I'm asking you so I won't have to break in a new dance partner. If I remember correctly, we always managed to get that right."

She remembered how they'd danced, too. Pressed so closely together, they could've shared the same skin.

"But, if you won't go, I'll have to ask someone else."

That startled her. "Who?"

Zach frowned thoughtfully, then said, "Maybelle Parker. She was the auctioneer, so she probably didn't bid on anyone."

To her surprise, Kristin found herself laughing, and after the night she'd had, it felt good. "You're joking. Maybelle Parker will eat you alive."

"Ah, an even better reason to call her." He got up from the table and looked around. "Phone book?"

He wouldn't do it. Maybelle was ten years older and ten pounds heavier than he was, most of that chest. "Top drawer to the right of the sink. And you're not really going to call her."

Zach opened the drawer, consulted the book, then put it back.

Kristin started to believe. "All right, I'll think about it," she said, annoyed with herself for caving in to him.

"Think fast. I'm on my way to the phone."

"It's after eleven o'clock," she said in exasperation. "You're not calling anyone at this hour."

He tapped in a number, then held the receiver out so she could hear that it was ringing.

"Maybelle?" he said after a moment. "It's Zach Davis. Fine, thanks, you? Good. No, I'm back again. Yes, it is. I was just about to get to that. I was wondering if you'd—"

Kristin leapt off her chair and fought him for the receiver, but he kept it away from her. He covered the mouthpiece. "Are you going?"

"Yes!" she rasped. "Now hang up!"

Instead he placed the receiver in her hand and said with a grin, "See you Saturday night. Wear something sexy."

Kristin glared at him, then closing her eyes, took a deep breath and brought the phone to her ear. She'd make up something. She'd say Zach was calling to ask where and what time they were supposed to meet for the cruise.

She didn't have to say anything because Maybelle

Parker wasn't on the line. The number he'd dialed was the time and temperature.

Kristin slammed the receiver back on the hook and strode into the living room, then the foyer, searching for him. She yanked open her front door. He was just making the turn out of her driveway, his taillights red in the foggy darkness.

She watched until the fog swallowed him up, then slowly, closed and bolted the door. She sank back against it. What was she getting herself into? And why couldn't she make a decision where he was concerned and *stick* to it?

A tiny voice in her mind answered, *Because he was worried about you driving in the fog. Because he was so furious with Chad. And because he went to such lengths to convince you to go on the cruise.*

Kristin hugged herself, hating the hope that insisted upon creeping in. He'd made her laugh, and he'd made her warm when a thick pile robe hadn't been able to chase her chills away. He'd even poured her tea.

Straightening, she strolled wearily back to the kitchen to dump out the two cups neither of them had really wanted, then turned off the light. Whether he'd asked out of pity or some sense of chivalry, she would go with him, and she would dance with him the way they once had.

Because he'd be gone soon enough…then all she'd have left were memories.

Chapter 13

Edgy and conflicted, Zach sat in his idling truck, every muscle in his body coiled as he stared up through the fog at Hollister's lavish brick home. He wanted to rearrange Chad's face in the worst way, yet here he sat. Because he'd told Kristin he wouldn't touch the jerk.

You promised, she'd said. *Can I trust you to keep your word or not?*

He sighed impatiently. He'd known what she was thinking. She might have said that the past was behind them now, but she hadn't meant it. He would pay forever for his mistake, yet she'd forgiven a raving egomaniac like Chad. No justice there.

Muffled voices carried on the night air, alerting Zach that Hollister had company. He rolled down his window a little more. Somewhere beyond the thick stand of pines, an engine sprang to life.

The way he saw it, he had two choices. He could

hang back until the visitor left and read Hollister the riot act...or he could drive away and forget the whole thing.

Headlights poked through the fog and trees, and a vehicle came down the long, paved driveway.

Frowning, Zach drove on. Leaving without pounding Chad into the pavement grated on his nerves, but it was time he proved to Kris that his word meant something.

The chief's midnight visitor was still behind Zach when he turned onto Wisdom's main street. When he passed Eli's bookstore and Kristin's burned-out shop and saw the yellow caution tape still surrounding what was left of it, he felt a hollow spot open in his heart. Again, he thought that she didn't deserve that.

The car behind him picked up speed, probably because visibility was better in town than it had been on the outskirts. The sedan swung left on an intersecting lane—Grace Street. Curious, Zach turned left onto the street that ran parallel to Grace. He sped to the end of the block. He was in a residential area now, and he braked at the stop sign when he saw that the dark sedan had made a right turn and was coming toward him.

The car passed under the streetlight. Zach stared in surprise at the bitter face of the gray-haired, spectacled man behind the wheel. Then the car whizzed past, and if he'd been unsure of the driver's identity before, looking at the vanity license plate erased all doubt: TAX-MAN.

Tax man? What had Harlan Greene been doing at Hollister's house this late at night? Zach would've expected the old codger to be counting sheep at this hour.

Frowning, he headed back to the farmhouse. He considered Harlan's midnight ride for a while, but in the way that one thought sparks another, he ended up recalling the old man buying cinnamon rolls at Kristin's shop. Then his mind was filled only with her and the upcoming cruise. An eagerness he knew he shouldn't be feeling zipped along his nerve endings.

For a man who hadn't been excited about a woman in a long time, that little zip felt damn good.

The dining room of the *River Rose* was noisy and filled to capacity with bachelors and bachelorettes in formal eveningwear. Laughing and talking, they filed out onto the dance floor as the music started.

Kristin's pulse quickened as Zach pushed away from the candlelit table. The black tuxedo he wore tonight contrasted sharply with the crisp white linens on the tables. It couldn't hide his blatant masculinity. Not with his thick hair shagging over his collar, and steel-gray eyes calling up visions only whispered about in polite society. He was so tall, so broad through the shoulders, so uncompromisingly male. Zach extended his hand, and Kristin gave him hers.

This was the moment she'd looked forward to all evening. Dinner was over, waiters in white tuxes were clearing away their dessert plates and coffee cups, and the music was low and dreamy, a perfect complement to the dimmed crystal chandeliers and tiny twinkle lights glimmering from posts and greenery.

Hand in hand, they moved to a quiet corner of the dance floor, and his appreciative gaze took her in. Her long white spaghetti-strap dress left her shoulders bare and skimmed her body, and tiny white sequins glittered from her bodice to her hem. When his attention moved to the side slit that ran from her left knee to the floor, he smiled. He even seemed to like the criss-crossed straps on her open-toed white heels.

"I know I told you to wear something sexy," he said, taking her in his arms. "But this…this is above and beyond anything I'd hoped for. Every man in this room wants to be me."

Laughing and demurring, Kristin slipped her arms around his neck and he brought their bodies close. It felt wonderful.

"First time you've worn this?" he asked.

"Why?"

"Because I don't want you to have worn it for anyone else."

Kristin smiled. Everything about this fantasy night pleased and delighted her, made her feel special. "It's new."

"New for me?" he asked smugly.

Refusing to add to his ego, she answered, "No, new for me."

Laughter rustled in his throat as he spun her even farther away from the crowd, the molding of their bodies awakening every primitive urge Kristin remembered. She was aware of everything about him. The strength in his hands, the faint dampness at the back of his collar where her hand rested, the knee that nudged the inside of her leg and asked her to glide with him, to feel.

And she would feel. She would throw caution to the winds because this night wasn't real. It was a fairy tale that seemed to say there would be no consequences in the morning, and they were free to go where the evening took them.

Chad and Mary Alice Hampton swung near, and

Kristin had to hide her disappointment at the intrusion. His smile was warm and friendly, but that was no surprise. She and Chad had managed to get their relationship back on shaky footing the day he'd come by to discuss Anna Mae's journals.

"Warm in here tonight," Chad called. "Even with the air-conditioning. Good thing dinner was decent."

Zach's glowering expression said he had no intention of speaking, so Kristin rushed to reply over the music. "It was delicious," she called. "Coq au vin's one of my favorite dishes."

"Mary Alice is one of mine," he joked and wiggled his brows.

"Oh, please," Mary Alice groaned. Then the slender blonde gave Chad a fun-loving shove toward the center of the crowd, and laughing, they spun away.

"You still speak to that slime?" Zach grumbled as they moved to the music again.

"He made a mistake, Zach."

"It was a big one."

"I know that. He knows it, too, and he's apologized a dozen times. I won't make him pay for it for the rest of his life."

Zach's gaze darkened, and she knew he was making comparisons between his mistake and Chad's. But she'd already told him the past was the past. There was no need to bring it up again. "Thank you for staying away from him that night."

"I promised, didn't I?"

He'd promised to love her forever, too, and that promise hadn't been too difficult to break.

"Actually," he continued in the same disgruntled tone, "I did drive out there after you told me what he'd done. But I didn't storm the house. He had company.''

''And if Chad had been alone?'' she asked, feeling a new jab of betrayal.

''I still would've driven away. I didn't back off because he had company, I backed off because when I give my word, I keep it.''

But he'd still gone out there, hadn't he?

The band finished the slow song to scattered applause, and they clapped along with the others. Zach met her eyes again, a curious look there. ''Guess who Hollister's company was?''

''I don't know. Who?''

''Harlan Greene.'' Zach stared at her for a few seconds, then said, ''You don't seem surprised.''

''I'm not. Chad told me he'd spoken to Harlan after he read Anna Mae's journal entries.''

''And?''

''And after reading the journals and examining all the evidence, he doesn't think Harlan—or anyone else—caused her death.''

''He still thinks it was an accident?''

''As he reminded me, that's how the coroner saw it, too. He did open a new investigation based on what Anna Mae had written, though. He said she tended to be a bit dramatic, but he'd never known her to lie. If she thought this man was up to something illegal, he probably was.''

''Midnight at the home of the chief of police is still a strange time and place to conduct an interview. Does everyone in this town jump when the chief speaks?''

The music began again, and Kristin pressed a fingertip to his lips to stop his grumbling. Her stomach flopped over when he touched his tongue to it.

With a wary look at him, she continued. "Maybe Chad questioned him at home to save Harlan's reputation. A few days ago, Bertie Patterson—one of Anna Mae's neighbors—saw someone go inside the house. Chad found Harlan there, looking for a keepsake. Questioning him at the office a second time might've started people talking again."

Kristin softened her voice, still feeling a tingle at the tip of her index finger. "Zach, let's not talk about Anna Mae and Harlan anymore. Let's just enjoy the night."

"Good idea," he said, bringing her close again. He didn't want to talk about them either. Not when she was so soft and pliant in his arms. Not when all he could think about was how well they moved together.

They stayed like that for a long time, through several slow songs. Then as they were leaving the dance floor, two merchants he'd met earlier called to Kristin and she excused herself to talk with them.

"I won't be long," she said.

"Take your time," he replied. "We have all night."

Ambling over to their table, Zach accepted the last glass of white wine from a passing waiter, then undid the black bow tie at this throat and stuck it in his pocket. He freed the top button on his shirt. Chad was a waste, but he'd been right about one thing. It was hotter than hell in here. And every time he looked at Kristin in that shimmering dress, the temperature rose another ten degrees.

As he sipped from his glass, Zach studied her classic features, watched the way she interacted with her friends. It was the first time since the fire that he'd seen her with anyone but Chad, and it was obvious that she honestly liked people. And they liked her.

There was a kindness, a grace, a genuine warmth about her.

He had friends, but he'd never had the whole-hearted, giving nature that she had. He'd always been too guarded, too worried about what people were thinking. Big surprise, he thought wryly. It wasn't as though he'd had a role model in Hap Davis. Where most people smiled and offered a hand*shake,* Hap had spent most of his life whining and asking for a hand-*out.*

Kristin eased away from her friends, then walked back to him. Every tiny sequin caught the light… sparkled over her breasts and hips. Zach's gut tightened.

She smiled as she reached him. "Remember when we were talking earlier, and Bob and Matt suggested we have another fund-raiser for the kids before Christmas?"

"Yep." He offered her his wineglass, and she accepted.

"Thanks. They think a locally televised auction on Halloween day might be fun. The hosts would dress in costumes and hand out treats to anyone who drops by the station to make a bid."

"Interesting," he said, not really interested at all. He got a weak feeling in the pit of his stomach as she sipped from his glass. As if she did it all the time.

Kristin handed it back. "We think we can get enough merchants to donate prizes, here and in Lancaster." Her dark eyes teased. "I might even ask a certain out-of-state contractor for a donation."

Zach grinned, liking the way she looked at him. "You want a couple of two-by-fours?"

"We want whatever he's willing to give," she said softly.

The temperature bumped up again. Zach knew she felt it, too. "Would there be incentives for him to donate?"

"That depends," she returned, eyes teasing. "What does he want?"

What did he want? He wanted her. He wanted more of the electric charge between them, more of the visceral pull that turned him inside out. But they were on a riverboat in the middle of Lake Edward. It would be hours before they moored and he could answer her truthfully. If then. Staring down into her eyes, he said quietly, "Right now, all he wants is to dance with you."

Kristin took the wineglass from his hand and put it on the table, then backed slowly onto the dance floor. She smiled softly. "I think that can be arranged."

The stars were diamond chips in the black sky, the June night warm and balmy when the *River Rose* docked a little after midnight. Anticipation spiced the air, along with the tension that hadn't let up since she'd drifted into his arms.

Zach tried not to hurry her as they walked in silence to the car. Then he seated Kristin and strode around to the driver's side of his aunt's dated, but impeccably kept white New Yorker. He and Etta had swapped vehicles earlier in the day. There was no way he would've asked Cinderella to ride to the ball in a contractor's truck. Not the way she looked tonight.

Zach slid under the steering wheel, shut the door and turned the key. The Chrysler's engine caught and he felt the car's slight vibration beneath him.

"I don't know how to say this, except to just say

it," he murmured. "I don't want to take you home just yet."

"Good," she said. "Because I don't want to *go* home just yet."

Zach dropped the car into gear and drove.

An hour later, a fire blazed beside Etta's pond, bright flames licking upward against a backdrop of dark trees and night sky. They lounged on his oversize sleeping bag, her bottom settled comfortably between the spread of Zach's thighs, his shoulders braced against the wooden bench near the water.

Kristin snuggled back against him, loving the feel of his arms around her. Earlier, they'd laughed when she'd emerged from Etta's bathroom in his navy sweat suit and white athletic socks. Now the mood was mellow as she considered the night and their part in it.

"You're almost finished here, aren't you?"

"Just about." His voice was deep and low behind her. "I have four or five days of work left. I need to install a couple of porch lights and railings...do some painting. I figure whoever buys the house can take care of all the fancy stuff."

Only four or five days? She'd known time was growing short, but— "I guess you'll be glad to get back."

"It's home. And Dan's been running the business single-handedly for too long. He has a family. He needs to spend time with them."

But there was no joy in his words. In fact, Kristin thought she heard a trace of regret. "Can I ask you something?"

"Shoot."

"Why is the business so much more important than the other things you want? You mentioned kids...and you have the sketch of that beautiful home in your room. You understand that Dan needs time with his family, yet…"

"Yet I don't even look for one myself?"

"Yes."

"Can't have a family without security. At least I can't."

"Zach, you're barely thirty-three, you own your own company and, from what you've said, it's doing well." She moistened her lips. "At least, it seemed that way when I was at your beach house. Isn't that enough?"

He fell silent for a moment, then he said, "I don't want a company that does well, Kris. I want a company that leaves everyone else's in the dust. There's security, and then there's success. My goal hasn't changed since I left here. In fact—" He paused again. "In fact, it's time I was honest with you."

She waited, motionless. "About what?"

"About us. You made the right decision not to leave with me after graduation. It would've never worked out. I had too much to prove, and the only way I could do it was by working my butt off."

She didn't speak, and he went on.

"It would've been even worse if we'd had kids. I would've worked even longer hours, and you would've been raising them alone." His arms were crossed above her breasts, and he tightened his hold on her. "I can't bring kids into the world until I can give them everything they need."

Kristin took his hands, regret creeping in for the child he'd been before Etta welcomed him into her home. "Kids need more than material things," she said quietly. "They need love and affection and a dad who'll be there for them."

"That will never be a problem for me," he said.

Wouldn't it? She wondered if he'd ever be able to alter his intense lifestyle, children or not. Habits—work ethics—were difficult to break when a man had been practicing them for his entire adult life. He was different here in Wisdom, more relaxed, more at ease. But she'd seen the transformation that came over him in Nags Head, and it wasn't attractive. Work was his life. His everything.

"Anyway," he concluded, "I just wanted you to know that you made the right decision back then. Both times."

Kristin stared into the fire and doubted that. She'd made decisions that had cost her the only man she'd ever loved. Yet she'd made the only decisions she could have at the time. First for an education that could have made their lives easier, then for her mother and herself. She'd wanted every spare second with her mother that she could have. Zach hadn't understood because he'd never known that kind of bond with anyone. And that thought only increased Kristin's sadness.

She turned to trace his cheek and mouth with a finger, and Zach's serious gray gaze locked on hers. He took her finger into his mouth. Then one of them released a shuddering breath and slowly, they began to touch, to explore. Zach's lips covered hers softly, gently searching, and Kristin slid her hand into his hair to bring him closer. It lasted a long time and ended sweetly.

The love she felt for him swelled in her chest and radiated outward until it filled every part of her. But it was bittersweet in light of what he'd just told her.

He would still be leaving. And wasn't that best for her, too?

"Hey," he murmured. "Let's take a dip in the pond."

"I already have most of your clothes. Are you offering me swimming trunks now?"

"Nope," he said, smiling. "Not even if I'd brought swimming trunks along."

There was no indecision, no hesitation. Kristin rose and slipped the sweatshirt over her head. She felt the warmth of the fire on her skin as she dropped the shirt to the ground.

Then Zach stood, too, his hands gentle as he stroked the sides of her breasts, then moved lower to slide the baggy sweatpants easily over her hips to pool at her feet. Kristin stepped out of them, slipped off her socks. Then all that remained were the white lace bikini briefs she'd worn with her dress. When he bent to take them off, the kiss he nuzzled to her breasts turned her knees to butter.

Zach stepped back to strip off his own clothes and drop them to the ground.

He was beautiful in the light of the fire, flickering shadows boldly outlining every long, straight limb, every corded muscle and sinew. Something tugged sweetly below Kristin's navel, but at the same time, a tiny voice in her mind whispered a warning. *He's going to hurt you again, and you have only yourself to blame.*

I know, she answered silently. *But sometimes love makes the only choice it can.*

"Ready for that dip?"

She smiled. "I'm ready for something, but I don't think it's water."

"Me, too," he answered through a chuckle. "But I guess that's pretty apparent." Drawing her close, he kissed her softly. "But let's make it last. I want to remember this night for a long time."

Kristin swallowed the lump in her throat and nodded. They would both have to rely on memories.

The pond was warm. They dunked each other, played like children, bobbed and splashed and kissed in water that came to Kristin's shoulders. She smiled as Zach flicked his tongue over droplets that clung to her lips. But as the moon climbed higher in the sky, their laughter ceased, and familiar hands beneath the surface of the water did exquisite things to her body. They relearned her curves and hollows...made her tremble inside.

Kristin let her hands rove where they would, too, exploring everything within her reach as she pressed kisses to his collarbone and felt him shudder. It wasn't long before his mouth claimed hers with crushing urgency. Water swelled and splashed as he jerked his hands under her thighs and brought her legs up to circle his waist.

"So much for swimming," she said through a throaty laugh.

His low laughter joined hers. "Swimming's overrated anyhow. Let's get out of here before we both drown."

Zach sloshed out of the water with Kristin still wrapping him securely, and slowly, he lowered them both to the sleeping bag. When he settled on top of her, he kissed her deeply. Deeper still, then sheathed himself in her warmth.

In the pond, he'd wanted her fast and hard. Now

that they were here beside the fire, he wanted her slowly…he wanted her gently.

Zach raised himself on his elbows to brush back her bangs. Then with a tenderness that took him completely by surprise, he kissed her forehead and eyelids, kissed her nose and her pretty, puffy mouth.

He looked down at her, seeing her sweetness and her unselfishness, her courage and her strength in the face of so much misfortune. And suddenly, his heart was so full, he could scarcely breathe. He wanted to tell her everything he needed, everything he feared. And she was both. But her dark eyes were turning liquid in the firelight, and her features were softening in a way that said it was the wrong time for talking.

Zach's heart thudded in his chest as he felt her take all that he was and ever hoped to be, and a real fear rose in him that he might never get that back. Then it was too late to worry about it because the drums were beating in his brain, his tempo was increasing and, with a low groan, he was carrying them both to paradise.

They lay silently for a time, waiting for the shuddering to stop and their breathing to level out.

Presently, Zach rolled away, then rose slightly to pull the flap of the sleeping bag over them. He grinned as Kristin nuzzled her nose into his chest hair and teased groggily, "Afraid your aunt Etta will come roaring up the driveway in your truck and find us like this?"

"Nope, I don't want to feed the mosquitoes." Settling down beside her, he snuggled her close and smiled. It felt like the clock had been turned back and they were kids again. It felt good. "Hey…want to get dressed and raid a few gardens?"

She laughed softly. "Feeling like a juvenile delinquent again?"

"I had a lot of fun when I was a juvenile delinquent. If we get caught and someone calls the cops, I'll pay the fine."

"Absolutely not. We're responsible adults now. We buy our vegetables."

"Didn't stop you thirteen years ago."

"We weren't responsible adults then."

She was burrowing into his chest again, bringing back that nice, tingly feeling. The feeling headed south. "Okay, killjoy," he said through a sigh. "What do responsible adults do after they've made love?"

Kristin rolled agilely on top of him, her legs like silk as they laced through his. "They do it again," she whispered, and settled in for a long, deep kiss.

Chapter 14

Troubled, Zach looked down on Kristin as she lay beside him on the cheap department-store futon. Her breathing was slow and steady and her expression, contented. He wished to God that he felt that relaxed. When they'd come inside last night, they'd used the dry side of his sleeping bag to cover up with. Now, it lay low on her shoulder, leaving the tops of her breasts open to the morning sun streaming through the windows. Even with a slight mascara smudge below her lashes, she was beautiful. But he was too churned up to fully appreciate it.

Last night, they'd made love twice without protection. *Twice.* He hadn't worried after they'd been together on the beach. What were the chances she'd get pregnant after sleeping with him only once? But this time... What an idiot he was. What idiots they *both* were.

Unless she was on the pill. That would explain her

lack of concern about having sex without a condom. And she *hadn't* been concerned. He would have sensed it if she was.

Warming to the idea, he felt the knots in his stomach ease. In this day and age, intelligent women took care of themselves, didn't they? Kris was no dummy. Besides, he'd told her enough times that he wasn't ready for fatherhood or anything close to it. She wouldn't deliberately try to deceive him. She was too honest and she had too much class.

Satisfied that he had everything figured out, Zach looked down at her again, and this time he smiled at the view. She really was beautiful.

The roar of an engine and grinding gears jerked Kristin awake at the same time Zach sat upright. He swore beneath his breath.

"Etta?" she asked, wide-eyed.

"She must be here for her car."

Kristin threw back the sleeping bag and hurried to grab her dress and panty hose from the chair while Zach snagged his jeans from the hardwood floor. He thrust both legs in at the same time, then lunged to his feet to yank them up.

Two doors slammed out in the driveway—not one—and he swore again. If it were any other woman running around in her underwear he wouldn't care. Well, he'd care a little. But this was Kris, and he didn't want people gossiping about her.

"Etta has someone with her," he said in a rush, scooping up her white heels and adding them to her pile. "Better lay low till I get rid of them." Then without thinking, he kissed her and hurried to the door, zipping his fly and digging in his front pocket for Etta's keys.

Nonstop chatter accompanied the clunk of ortho-
pedic shoes as the two women climbed the stairs and
crossed the porch. He opened the door before Etta had
the chance.

"Why, good morning, dear!" Etta exclaimed
brightly. She tipped her cheek up for his kiss as she
entered. "You remember Bertie Patterson, don't
you?"

Before he could say he remembered Mrs. Patterson,
they marched inside, silky dresses swishing all the way
into the living room. Apparently hats with flowers and
netting were still in style because Bertie and Etta wore
them proudly.

Etta's smile collapsed in a hurry when her gaze
darted from his spongy futon and sleeping bag to the
lamp and old wooden rocker he'd found in the attic.
"Oh, Zachary..." she moaned in dismay.

"It's fine, Aunt Etta."

"But it's so dreadfully *empty!*"

"It's convenient. I'll only be here another few days,
and I won't have a lot of junk to put away before I
take off. Now what brings you ladies by this morning?
Heading out to church?"

Bertie nodded enthusiastically. "We're breaking in
a new minister."

"But I need to pick up my car beforehand," Etta
said. "Bertie has a hard time climbing in and out of
your truck, and we're going visiting after church."

Bertie peered up sweetly through her Coke-bottle
glasses. "Did you and Kristin enjoy the movie last
night?"

Confused, Zach glanced at Etta. "Movie?"

Etta shook her head and spoke a little louder. "He

didn't take her to the movies, Bertie. It was a *dinner cruise*."

"Oh!" Bertie said, flustered. "Gracious, I'm getting as deaf as that strange Arnett woman." She stuck a finger in her ear and cranked up her hearing aid. "I thought you said they were seeing a *Tom Cruise* film."

"No, dear. And I doubt Mrs. Arnett's deaf," Etta said, keeping her voice raised. "I believe that son of hers just likes to yell."

"You'd think they'd be a little kinder to each other on a Sunday morning," Bertie declared.

"Indeed I would."

The mention of the Arnetts sharpened Zach's interest. "Mrs. Arnett and her son are back in town?"

Etta nodded. "When I picked up Bertie, the two of them were across the street at Anna Mae's house, one hollering louder than the other." Her raised brows and knowing tone said the Arnetts were up to no-good. "They had a small U-Haul in the driveway."

"Mrs. Arnett owns the house, Aunt Etta. She's entitled to take what she wants from it."

"Oh, they weren't taking anything," Bertie piped up. "They were bringing it all back."

Bringing it back? Zach slashed another look at Etta.

"The Mrs. never stepped a foot inside the house," Bertie continued. "Just watched her boy drag box after box inside. It was plain that *she* wanted everything returned, but *he* had other ideas."

"True enough," Etta said, then frowned at the old-fashioned timepiece dangling from a pin on the front of her dress. "Oh, dear. We'd better move along before we're late. Zachary, I need my keys. Yours are in your truck."

"Here you go," he said, dropping them into her hand.

She thanked him, then startled him by stepping close and lowering her voice again. "Tell Kristin goodbye for me. I assume it's her perfume I'm smelling, not yours." Her eyes twinkled at his slack-jawed look, and she added in a stage whisper, "Now don't mess it up this time."

Then, while he was still trying to come up with a reply, she patted his cheek affectionately and herded Bertie out the door.

When Kristin walked into the room a moment later dressed in his sweats again, Zach turned to her and shrugged. "She smelled your perfume."

Not much got by Etta, Kristin thought, smiling. "Do you care?" She'd made a decision to be with him last night, and she only had one regret—that this was an affair, nothing more.

"No, I'm a big boy. If you're worried that she'll tell anyone else, though, don't be. She likes you. Did you hear the whole conversation?"

"Most of it. The Arnetts are back. Zach, I need to go home and change, then see Chad. When I asked Mildred if she wanted Anna Mae's journals—" She stopped when his gaze abruptly cooled. "Is something wrong?"

"Not that I know of," he said, flashing a new grin and moving to the chair where his laundry was stacked. He grabbed a pair of clean socks. "Finish your thought."

Frowning and wondering if she'd imagined that fleeting look, she went on. "I was going to say that Mildred has this notion that nothing should've been taken from the house. I think I told you she's into psychic readings. She's sure Anna Mae started the fire at my shop.''

Zach rolled his eyes and sank to the futon to pull on his socks.

''I know, but she believes it. Now that she's returning Anna Mae's things, I think Chad should search the house for those photographs. They could be inside something the Arnetts brought back. If we hurry, we can see Mildred before she leaves. There's even a chance that she found them and not realized they were important.''

''Fine,'' he said casually. ''Give me a minute to finish dressing, and I'll drop you off at home.''

Kristin paused as his words sank in. Was he distancing himself again? ''Don't you want to go with me?''

''Thanks, but I can't.'' He took a T-shirt from the stack and pulled it over his head, then flashed another grin at her. ''I need to get some work done. I'll leave the ghost chasing to you and Hollister.''

''Zach?''

''Do you need a bag for your clothes?'' he asked, then before she could answer, walked into the kitchen and raised his voice to be heard. ''I think there's one around here somewhere.''

Kristin stared after him, feeling a combination of hurt and bewilderment. Was he annoyed that she'd mentioned Chad after the night and morning they'd spent together? If so, why would he care? He'd not only told her he'd be leaving in a few days, he'd said the same thing to his aunt mere minutes ago.

Coming back into the living room, Zach handed her a plastic grocery bag. ''Here you go. This should be

big enough.'' Then he dropped to the futon again to
tug on his boots.

Suppressing a sigh, Kristin slipped her gown inside
the bag, then wriggled her feet into her white heels.
When they left a few minutes later, her mood was
more conflicted than her outfit.

Her spirits were still low forty minutes later when
she pulled in behind Mildred Arnett's U-Haul and got
out. Zach wasn't the only reason she was out of sorts.
When she got home, there'd been a message from
Chad on her answering machine. He wanted her to go
to Tuesday night's annual Fraternal Order of Police
dinner, where he'd be speaking. She dreaded calling
him back.

Kristin walked up to Mildred's open window and
found her nervously chewing her lip. Before she could
say hello, a patrol car pulled up to the curb with Larry
McIntyre behind the wheel. Seconds later, Chad pulled
in behind him.

"Mildred, what's going on?" Kristin asked. "Why
are the police here?"

The woman's eyes bulged fearfully, her frizzy white
hair practically standing on end. "Will found some of
Anna Mae's frogs smashed in the basement. I told him
there was no use reporting a break-in—she did it herself to let us know she was upset. But Will called them
anyway. What can the police do? They have no juris-
diction over the wills of the spirits. I thought returning
the things we took would make everything all right,
but—"

"Where's your son now, Mildred?"

She pointed at the house. "In there."

Kristin's mind raced. Frogs had been smashed? Had

the photographs been inside one of Anna Mae's favorite knickknacks? A few of them *had* been large enough, but how would she cut through the hollow figurines without ruining— Then she remembered the large frog bank on Anna Mae's dresser. *Banks already had an opening.*

With a comforting squeeze to Mildred's arm, Kristin tempered her excitement and moved to the walk beside the front door to meet Chad and Larry. She wanted to talk to them out of Mildred's earshot.

Chad reached her first. "What are you doing here?"

"Long story," she replied. "I'll explain later."

He seemed to accept her answer because he nodded toward the U-Haul and changed the subject. "Are they both in the truck?"

"No, Will's inside."

Chad turned to Larry. "Go ahead and get started with Mr. Arnett. I'll talk to his mother and be right in."

"Sure. See you in there."

When Larry was gone, Chad glanced toward the U-Haul again. "What's her story today?"

"She thinks Anna Mae smashed the figurines because her things were taken from the house. She also believes her cousin started the fire at my shop for the same reason. Which is why Mildred brought back the pieces she took."

"Busy ghost," Chad said dryly.

"Chad, I came over here because there's a chance the snapshots Anna Mae wrote about in her journals are inside something Mildred returned. That is, *if* they weren't in the frogs that were smashed. If you search the house—really search it from top to bottom—"

He stared blankly. "Do you know how much manpower that would take? Talk about your needles in haystacks. We'd be looking for a three or four-inch square of paper in a three-story house that's cluttered to the rafters. We're a small department, Kristin, and we're busy. Besides the day-to-day stuff and these nuisance calls, I'm up to my ears in the drug case.''

"This isn't a nuisance call," she said insistently. "What if the person who smashed the frogs really *was* involved in Anna Mae's death? You have to believe that something's going on now. Anyone looking for valuables to sell for drugs wouldn't give frog figurines a second look, much less break them for sport.''

Chad assessed her for several long moments, indecision churning through his green eyes. Finally, he said, "Did you get the message I left on your answering machine?''

Biting back the urge to ask what that had to do with the break-in, Kristin braced herself for an argument. "Yes," she replied calmly, "but I don't think that's a good idea.''

Chad's easy grin took her by surprise. "It's not what you think. I wanted to ask Mary Alice, but she'll be out of town Tuesday night. Asking a woman I've dated could mess things up with her.''

The weight on her shoulders shifted a little. "You and Mary Alice—?''

"—got along *very* well last night. I know it's early, and I shouldn't be thinking this way, but...I really like her. I don't want to screw this up by asking someone else to the dinner, and I don't want to go alone.''

Kristin's relief was only surpassed by the happiness she felt for him. Sometimes wishes did come true. "Oh, Chad that's wonderful.''

"So—" he said, getting back to his invitation,

"—we'd be going to dinner as friends. *Just* friends. *Only* friends. Nothing *but* friends."

Still, Kristin hesitated, Zach's tenderness and warmth over the past day fueling her reluctance.

"Okay," Chad said, "I'll put it another way. You scratch my back, and I'll scratch yours." He gestured at Anna Mae's home. "I'll have Larry look around today, and I'll finish on Friday when I'm off. I'll give you the whole day—if you'll give me a few hours on Tuesday night."

She couldn't say no. The search was too important. "Chad, I could help, too," she blurted. "I saw a bank in her bedroom that was large enough—"

"Sorry. But if we do find something, there could be chain-of-evidence problems if I allowed you inside a crime scene."

Crime scene? He was no longer dubbing it a nuisance call? "You think there's something funny going on, now, too, don't you?"

"Yeah," he said through a sigh. "I do. Dammit."

On Monday morning, as Kristin prepared to leave for Jeremy Sherwood's office in Lancaster, she mulled over the conversation she'd had with Chad last night. He'd found the bank Kristin mentioned smashed in the basement, along with the chalky remains of four other figurines. There was no sign of the photos, but the broken pieces would be dusted for fingerprints. Chad admitted, too, that the burglar had to have known Anna Mae to recognize the frogs as special possessions.

Slinging her white straw bag over her shoulder, she put on her second earring and headed for the door. When she opened it, Zach was just coming up the walk. She was stunned to see him looking so worn-out, dark smudges under his eyes.

"What's wrong?" she said, immediately concerned.

"I'm starving," he said through a broad grin. "Want to grab lunch somewhere?"

Having lunch with him would be wonderful, but... "Have you slept since you brought me home yesterday?"

"I got a few hours."

"But not many." From the looks of him, he'd worked through the night. Was he that eager to return home? He'd obviously showered and shaved, and instead of his work clothes, he wore a soft yellow polo shirt with his jeans. How a man could look tired and compellingly vital at the same time defied all logic.

He scanned her white tank top and mint green jacket and slacks. "I see you're ready. Where are we eating?"

Feeling a warm glow, Kristin locked the door behind her and headed for her van. "I don't know about you, but I'm having lunch in Lancaster. My architect has a few floor plans to show me."

"Lancaster works for me," he said, falling into step beside her. "Actually, I wouldn't mind looking at the plans. From a contractor's standpoint, I might be able to suggest a few things this guy didn't think of."

Kristin stared quizzically as he opened the passenger-side door of the van for her. He wasn't at all surprised that she was leaving for Lancaster, and his timing was perfect. *Was* this a spur of the moment invitation? Or had Zach remembered that she was seeing Jeremy this afternoon, and for some reason, wanted to go along? Of course, the next question she asked herself was, why?

Tired of trying to figure him out, Kristin climbed into the van, then gave him the same answer he'd given her when she'd offered to help with Etta's back porch. She handed him the keys. "Suit yourself."

The meeting with Jeremy was a disaster, and it was all Zach's fault. Kristin assessed his careless expression as they drove out of the lot at Sherwood Designs, and Zach turned onto Route 30.

"Was that necessary?" she asked.

Zach sent her an innocent look. "I think so. If we don't leave the parking lot, we'll never get to the restaurant, and I'm still hungry."

"Don't joke about this. The things you said to Jeremy were inexcusable."

Zach kept scanning the street, presumably for eateries. "No, the floor plans he showed you were inexcusable."

"There was nothing wrong with any of them. I didn't ask him for the Taj Mahal, I asked for a simple shop with three bays and some charm, and he did that."

"I just don't think you should rush into anything."

"I'm not planning to, but I have to start rebuilding soon to be open for Christmas." Kristin paused to calm herself. "I need some order in my life. I'm moving ahead as soon as possible."

"Whatever," he said, shrugging, but there was more than a trace of disapproval in his tone. "Now where would you like to eat?"

They chose a Pennsylvania-Dutch style family restaurant in nearby Smoketown, and sampled everything that was offered at the long table they shared with tourists from Ohio. It was down-home cooking with a variety of meats and noodle dishes, as well as regional favorites like chowchow and pepper cabbage. By the time their waitress set the shoofly and Dutch apple pies on the table and took orders for ice cream, neither of them had room for dessert.

Zach groaned through a chuckle as he squeezed behind the steering wheel. "Why did you let me eat so much?"

"A man needs fuel to work."

"This man could've done with a lot less of it." He started the engine. "Now what do you want to do?"

Kristin snapped on her seat belt, then studied him in surprise. "You're not ready to go home?"

Zach pulled out of the parking lot. "Nah. I think we should take a tour. The city's changed since I was here last." Two black Amish buggies passed by in the opposite lane, the horses clopping easily along the road. He grinned and recanted. "Well, maybe it hasn't changed that much."

Kristin leaned back against the headrest and closed her eyes. "I'm too full to tour. I need a nap."

"Oh, no you don't. Fair's fair. I gave you a tour when you were in Nags Head."

Her eyes flew open and she straightened. "You did not. I took myself on a tour, such as it was. All I saw was sand and water."

"Did you like it?"

"Yes, very much. Just not as much as I like it here."

"No?"

She shook her head. "It's beautiful. And at first, I was really swept away by all of it. Then I got back and realized that I'd missed seeing green trees and wheat fields." She smiled. "And Amish buggies. You know the old saying, 'It's a nice place to visit, but I wouldn't want to live there?' Well that about sums it up. This is where I belong. This is home.'' She glanced at him. "You know?"

Zach nodded somberly and drove.

They ended up touring anyway. They spent hours strolling through an open-air flea market where Kristin bought several woven baskets and a colorful Amish quilt. Then they stopped at a fruit stand for fresh raspberries. The tour ended at the wax museum in Lancaster.

It was nearly dark when they entered Wisdom's town limits, the mood inside the van, satisfied and contented, the summer air through the open windows laced with the smells of new things growing.

When Zach pulled into Kristin's driveway, shut off the engine and leaned over to kiss her deeply, it was expected, anticipated...and welcomed. The lure and tingle of attraction had been with them all day, running just below the surface.

Still, when their lips parted and he remained near, she had to ask why.

Zach's gaze drifted over her features. "Because you're beautiful and I've wanted to do that all day."

"Even at Jeremy's office?" she said through a quiet smile.

Zach unfastened his seat belt. "Especially at Jeremy's office."

The second kiss was even more thrilling than the first. The third had him releasing her seat belt, too, and pulling her as close to him as the console between the bucket seats would allow.

Everything in Kristin alternately sang and scolded, but the music won out. The wonderful day they'd spent together won out. His talented hands and lips won out.

They were both gasping for breath when Zach finally tore his mouth from hers and rasped, "The back of the van, or your bed?"

"My bed," she said through husky laughter, loving him, and feeling the wonder of it balloon inside of her. "Mrs. Franz would be scandalized if she found us groping each other in the driveway."

"No, she wouldn't," he said, kissing her neck, then moving lower to rub his nose and lips over her breasts above her tank top. "She'd be glad you were having a good time."

She smiled, cupping the back of his head. "Am I going to have a good time?"

He worked his way back up, raining kisses over her throat and chin. "Oh, yeah," he murmured, finding her lips again. "We both are."

How they got inside the front door without tripping and falling over each other was a minor miracle. How they managed to reach even the third step on the way to her second floor bedroom before they collapsed on the stairs was a major feat.

The kissing and touching reached new heights. Kristin kicked out of her sandals, wiggled her arms through the sleeves while Zach peeled off her jacket.

The phone rang.

His fevered whisper shivered through her as the phone rang again and he nuzzled her ear and hairline. "Let it ring."

She would've laughed if she hadn't been so aware of his hands unfastening the belt on her slacks. She had no intention of answering the phone. In fact, it was amazing that either of them had heard it with all the heavy breathing that was going on.

Zach yanked her belt from the loops and cast it aside, then moved his hands to the button on her waistband as the phone kept ringing.

The answering machine clicked on. A loud, hearty male voice spilled from the living room into the entryway.

"Kristin, it's Chad. Pick up if you're there."

Zach kissed her harder, deeper, popped the button through the buttonhole.

"Not there?" the disembodied voice said after a short pause. "Okay. I just wanted to tell you that I'll pick you up around seven-fifteen tomorrow night. I forgot to mention the time yesterday. Dinner's at eight at the Horseheads Inn, but retired Chief Nance is coming with his wife, and I know you like her. That'll give you and Emily a chance to visit before we eat." He finished with a smile in his voice. "I guess that's all. See you soon."

The click of the machine shutting off was almost deafening.

Zach levered himself off of Kristin with a hand on the step above her head, then backed away and released a blast of air. He didn't mince words. "You're having dinner with Chad?"

Kristin sat up, disturbed by the sudden coldness in the air. "It's not a real date. I'm only going with him because Mary Alice can't make it, and he doesn't want to mess things up with her by asking another woman."

"You're not 'another woman'?"

"I'm a friend."

The chill in Zach's gray eyes went right through her. "Why can't he go alone?"

"It's the annual police dinner, and he's speaking," Kristin replied, as if that explained everything. "Zach, it's only a dinner."

Though he nodded, a nerve continued to pulse at his jaw. "I just didn't expect you to see anyone else while I was still in town."

Kristin stilled for a very long moment as his words caromed around in her head. Then a feeling of hurt and anger erupted inside of her, along with a sickening feeling of being used. She stood, her voice starting out low and gaining momentum as she set him straight.

"You didn't expect me to see anyone else while you were here? Why do you even care? In less than a week, you'll be gone, and we'll both go on with our lives as before." She met his cold stare with one of her own. "Or were you planning to breeze into town to bed me every so often, then be on your way again? We don't have a monogamous relationship, Zach. We don't have any relationship at all. Who I see is my own business."

Zach's anger had kept pace with hers while she spoke. "Know what? You're absolutely right. Who you see *is* your own business. How stupid of me not to remember that." He strode to the door, throwing it open and stalking out on the porch. "By all means, see whoever you damn please!"

"I plan to!" she shot back.

The only reply she got from him was the gunning of his truck's engine as he tore out of her driveway.

Kristin slammed the inside door and climbed the stairs to the bathroom, sobs wracking her chest and tears falling. The six-mile drive would give him plenty of time to think about his stupid, asinine, ignorant remarks. But there was no forgiveness for him if he phoned to apologize tonight.

She didn't know when she'd finally forgiven him for being with Gretchen—for breaking her trust. Maybe it was on the cruise when he'd told her he hadn't gone after Chad because he'd made a promise to her. There'd been no specific marking of the event.

But this. This was the end of it. She was through wishing and hoping for a man who didn't respect her, didn't value her and didn't love her. Kristin stepped out of her slacks and stuffed them into the hamper. Etta had been right, she decided, pushing open the glass shower doors and turning on the spray. They'd needed closure. Now they had it.

Chapter 15

Kristin eased away from Larry McIntyre's chatty wife and returned to her table, tired of mingling. She sipped iced tea while she waited for Chad to finish talking with several out-of-town police officers. There was no shortage of them. The banquet room hummed with after-dinner conversation. Now that the evening was drawing to a close, she was eager to leave. Her cheeks ached from forcing smiles all night and pretending a lightness of heart she didn't feel. The one bright spot was talking with Emily Nance, who was charming, witty and unpretentious.

Kristin hid her uneasiness as councilman Len Rogers sent her another inebriated grin and shuffled toward her again. Waving, she made a beeline for the powder room. Len had been drinking steadily since he'd wandered into the banquet room from the bar to speak to Chad. Now, for some reason, he seemed to want her company.

It was nice to see Emily lazing on one of the powder room's mauve chairs, wiggling her toes. Her white pumps lay beside her on the floor.

"Uh-oh," Emily said, laughing. "Caught in the act." She motioned to her shoes. "New heels. I should know better. I tried to stick it out, but Hank never shuts up when he comes to these things, and dang it, my feet hurt." She looked at Kristin's thin high heels and shook her gray head. "How you young women manage to walk gracefully in those things is beyond me—never mind wearing them for hours."

Kristin grinned and took the chair beside her. "They aren't my favorites, but I bought them to go with this dress. Turquoise is hard to match." She paused. "Actually, I'm ready to go, too, but it looks like Chad and your husband have a lot in common."

Emily studied her for a moment, then said, "Forgive me for saying so, but I've been thinking that you've wanted to leave since you got here. There's no sparkle in those brown eyes tonight." Her tone softened. "Still upset about the fire?"

Yes, but it was Zach who had her more upset. Even though she had no intention of forgiving him, he hadn't called last night, and sleep had been a long time coming.

"I guess I'm a little distracted," Kristin replied. "Patience isn't one of my virtues, and I've had to wait for everyone under the sun for the go-ahead to clear my lot and start rebuilding. I got so antsy yesterday, I bought a few things to resell, even though I'll have to store them for a while."

"It was a shame you lost Anna Mae's pieces," Emily said, bending to massage her toes. "She had some lovely things. I didn't know her well, but her working for Hank gave us an opportunity to talk occasionally. She had a first edition Mark Twain that was in wonderful condition.''

But that was gone now, Kristin thought, along with the compassionate woman who'd purchased it.

"I don't suppose her hidey-hole survived?"

"Hidey-hole?"

Emily's smile turned to a wince as she wriggled back into her shoes. "That was what Anna Mae called it. It was an antique wooden chest about the size of a breadbox. Mahogany, I think—or maybe cherry. It had a hinged top and several narrow drawers running down the front, but there were also a few sliver-thin compartments that were nearly undetectable because of the way the wood was spliced together. It was one of her favorite pieces.''

Goose bumps cropped up on Kristin's arms. She'd seen that chest only days ago in her storage unit. But if it were one of Anna Mae's favorite pieces, why would she store it in the attic instead of keeping it nearby so she could enjoy it?

"Well, I'd better get out there and round up my fella," Emily said with a laugh. "If he's not ready to go, I'll read for a while." She patted her handbag where a book obviously resided. "I'm never without options.''

Kristin pushed to her feet as well. "I'll walk out with you. I need to find Chad." And she needed to examine that chest!

"Anything going on there?" Emily teased as they reentered the hall. "Or with the good-looking bachelor you bought at the auction?"

Kristin forced a wan smile. "No. Chad's just a friend, and Zach…" She tried to keep the disappointment from her voice. "Well, Zach's leaving in a few days. Nice talking with you, Emily."

"Same here," the older woman returned, eyeing her curiously. Then she half walked, half limped toward a group of officers where her husband was holding court.

Chad was just leaving his friends when Kristin reached his side. "Chad, I'm sorry, but I have to go. If you want to stay, that's fine. It's only a four block walk back to my apartment."

His forehead lined instantly. "What's wrong?"

"Nothing's wrong. Something might be right." Her conversation with Emily Nance rushed from Kristin like a dam bursting. Her excitement was contagious.

"You think you saw this chest?" Chad repeated.

"Yes, that's why I need to go out to the lake—to check the compartments. Chad, Anna Mae called it her 'hidey-hole'."

"I'm going with you. It's too dark and secluded out there at this time of night for you to go alone. Give me a couple of minutes to say my goodbyes and make sure Len's not driving himself home."

"Okay," she replied, glad for Chad's vigilance where Len was concerned. "He's been hitting the sauce pretty hard tonight."

"Not just tonight. He's been hitting it hard for quite a while."

Kristin shook her head, sorry to hear that. Then she nodded toward Emily who'd just taken a seat at one of the tables and pulled a paperback from her handbag. "I'll visit until you get back."

Zach stepped out of the shower and toweled off, his nerves on edge and a litany of curses banging around in his head. For the past twenty-four hours he'd been trying to drive her out of his mind—trying to center on the work and business that gave him so much pride and satisfaction. But every tick of the clock just brought her nearer. There was no use fighting it. He was in love with her all over again. That's why he was such a fault-finding horse's ass at the architect's office yesterday. And that's why he didn't want her rushing full-tilt to rebuild, or doing dinner favors for Hollister. He wanted her with him—wanted the dream of Kristin chasing that little replica of herself along the beach.

She won't move, a voice in his head said smugly. *She likes it right where she is, and right now, she doesn't like you at all.*

But she could change her mind, couldn't she? There had to be more going on between them than chemistry or she wouldn't get so ticked off at him every time he turned around.

Zach flung the towel over the shower rod and pulled on his clothes. He loved her and he needed her, and he was going to swallow his pride, take a chance on being rejected and drive out to the damn Horseheads Inn to grovel like a fool. He had to get to her before Chad convinced her that he was her future. Hollister's sudden attraction to Mary Alice Hampton was a fairy tale. No man in his right mind would look at another woman if he thought he had a snowball's chance in hell with Kris.

And he had less of a chance than that.

Fifteen minutes later, Zach passed Len Rogers as he strode through the taproom and entered the banquet hall. He looked around. There were only a dozen or so people left in the hall, most of them in uniform, and none of them, Hollister. He went back to the bar.

Rogers was three sheets to the wind, nursing a drink, and in a surly mood. Zach didn't have time for it. "I said," he repeated, "have you seen Hollister tonight?"

"Yeah, I saw 'im," Len grumbled after another sip from his rocks glass. "He came by to collec' my car keys and my little envelope." He snorted a mirthless laugh. "Which became *his* little envelope, jus' like always."

Zach frowned. "Envelope?"

Rogers eyed him hesitantly, then scowled and went back to his drink.

A big, burly officer in a brown uniform ambled over to them. "Did I hear you mention Chief Hollister? I'm looking for him, too."

The man's nametag said W. Schrecongost and Zach knew immediately that he had to be Hollister's cop friend from York. How many crime-fighting William Schrecongosts could there be in the area?

Len attempted to focus on the man, his head weaving. "You a good buddy of our illus...trious chief's?"

Schrecongost flicked an amused look at Zach, then answered Len. "Not really, but we generally see each other once a year at this thing. He took your keys, huh?"

"Took more'n that," Len muttered, slamming his empty glass down and moving uncertainly off his barstool. "Prob'ly selling my car right now." He flung a limp arm toward the banquet room as he staggered off. "He was talkin' to Nance's wife las' time I saw him. Maybe she knows where he is."

Schrecongost let out a long, low whistle. "Good thing he's walking tonight. He's really had it."

"You bet," Zach replied, but his mind was already back on Kristin. "You don't happen to know what Mrs. Nance looks like, do you?" He couldn't recall ever seeing her when he lived here.

"Yep. Nice woman. Gray hair, blue dress. She's the only barefoot reader in the room."

Moments later, Zach was standing over her. "Mrs. Nance?"

Looking up over her half glasses, she smiled wryly and glanced toward her husband. "For the moment at least. Do we know each other?"

"No. Councilman Rogers said you'd been talking to Chief Hollister. Is he still around?"

"No, he and his date left a few minutes ago."

Disappointed, Zach turned away. "Thank you. I'll try them at Kristin's."

"Wait, young man." Mrs. Nance studied his face for several long beats, then smiled. "Why, you're Etta Gardner's nephew, aren't you? The man Kristin bought at the auction."

Zach was startled until he remembered how small towns operated. Everyone knew everything about everybody. "Yes. And she's the one I need to talk to."

His admission seemed to delight the older woman. "Well, you won't find her at home. She and Chad went to her storage place to examine an antique chest."

"They're at Lakeside?"

"If that's where her storage bay is."

Calling his thanks, Zach hurried to his truck, unsettled as visions of Chad and Kristin swam in his mind. He could see them searching together, Chad playing the gallant supporter and Kris smiling her appreciation. But after a few moments, the visions started to make him crazy, and he had to blot them out.

He was nearly to Lake Edward when his preoccupation with her backed off just enough to let a few stray thoughts through. They hit him like a pile driver.

He searched his memory for two recent conversations he'd overheard, then he compared them with those he'd heard tonight. There were discrepancies in them. Big ones.

In the next instant, he shook his head. He was getting as bad as Kris with this amateur detective crap. Len's drunken rambling about envelopes was probably nothing, even though he'd seen Len give Chad an envelope at Kris's shop. And although Schrecongost had implied that he and Chad hadn't seen each other for a year, Hollister probably *had* been with the big cop the night of the fire. Schrecongost wasn't obligated to tell a stranger like Len anything—particularly that he and Chad were currently working a case together.

Still, Zach's mind continued to spin. Was Chad dirty? Was he accepting payoffs? And could Chad have been the "man she'd once cared about" in Anna Mae's journal? The man with the vicious temper?

Zach's heart pounded as he considered Chad's rash behavior the night he'd followed Kristin, and he pushed his boot down hard on the accelerator. He didn't like what he was thinking—couldn't trust it. But the damp prickles at the back of his neck wouldn't let him ignore the possibility that Kris was in trouble.

Eagerly, Kristin dropped to her knees and dug board games, puzzles and cards from the large cardboard carton, then set them in the middle of the floor to join wisps of packing material from her previous search. She lifted out the antique box and flashed a smile up at Chad, who stood over her. "Here it is! Keep your fingers crossed."

"Believe me," he said. "They're crossed."

Kristin ran her fingers lightly over the seams, looking for those two hidden drawers. Her heart leapt when she found them near the bottom, camouflaged in the trim. In a second both drawers were open and she was beaming.

"They're here!" she said excitedly. Quickly, she pulled out two snapshots and what appeared to be a letter. "Chad, look! Here's—" Shock nearly immobilized her. It quickly turned to stunned disbelief.

Slowly, Kristin inched back to sit on the sealed carton behind her. She couldn't believe her eyes. But there was no mistaking the identity of the man on the right.

She looked up at Chad again, the bare bulb overhead illuminating his grave expression. "Who's the man with you in these pictures?"

Sighing, he eased back against the tall boxes lining the left wall. "His name is Pax Lafarge. He's a dealer I picked up on drug charges about a year ago."

"And the envelope he's handing you?"

When he didn't answer, Kristin lifted the letter. "I imagine it's all written down here, but I'd rather hear it from you."

"It's gratitude money from some businessmen whose...enterprises...were saved because I had Lafarge make a phone call."

"What kind of phone call? And why would he do a favor for you?"

"I think you know," Chad returned in the same

beaten tone. "In exchange for Lafarge's telling the dealers they were about to be raided, I made sure that a kilo of cocaine with his prints on it disappeared from my evidence room. Pax knew that it could be 'found' again if he ever crossed me."

"Chad, why would you do such a thing? You're so wonderful with the kids. You go out of your way to warn and educate them about the dangers of drugs."

"The oldest reason in the book. Money."

"Money?" She got to her feet. "But I thought—"

"—that my parents left me well off? They did. But along with the house and other assets, they also left me an appreciation for the finer things in life. The money went fast. Taxes alone on that brick monstrosity damn near bankrupted me. Although," he added smugly, "I got a very nice reduction when I found out that Harlan likes to dress up in women's clothes and go clubbing in Philadelphia."

"You blackmailed Harlan?"

But he didn't appear to hear the question. "I did it all for you," he said, his face lining earnestly. "The glassed-in room for the hot tub, the in-ground pool, the state-of-the-art kitchen—I wanted the house to be perfect for you when we got married."

Kristin felt herself pale.

"I'd lost heavily in the market, and when I got a tip that tech stocks were going through the roof, I bought a ton of them on margin. I needed to recoup my losses." He paused. "The damn things sank faster than the *Titanic*. The brokers wanted their money, and I didn't have it. I had to do something, didn't I?"

"Did you even *consider* getting a loan from the bank?" she asked. "How did Anna Mae find out?"

He sent her a droll look. "My dear secretary accidentally opened some personal mail that was sent to the office—a notice from my broker saying they'd attach my wages, possibly my house, if I didn't pay up. She was full of apologies for opening it, but the damage was done. I couldn't have her running off at the mouth and destroying my standing in the community."

Chad's tone cooled. "I'm afraid I said some harsh things to her that day. When she left, she was...well, terrified." He nudged a clump of excelsior packing with the toe of his shoe. "I don't recall exactly what I said, but I figured she'd keep her mouth shut and stay the hell out of my business from that day on.

"But she didn't. The night she died, she told me that she'd been listening in on my phone calls. She knew I was getting money from Harlan and Len, and she knew I'd met Pax to pick up my...reward."

"Len, too?" she asked in dismay.

"After his last DUI, he should've done jail time. Jail's not a good thing for a councilman who wants to get reelected."

Harlan, Len...drug dealers? Dear God.

Chad nodded at the photos she held. "Anna Mae said she'd take those to the state police if I didn't turn myself in—said she wanted *me* to do it because she cared about me, and things would go easier on me if I went to them. Like hell she cared. She was scared and saying anything she could think of to diffuse the situation."

"Chad, did you hurt her?"

"No," he answered, and she could see that he was sincere. "I only wanted the pictures, but she wouldn't give them up. Not even when I told her that everything she had on me, including those snapshots, was circumstantial. I could've easily said that the money from Pax was part of a sting I'd set up to learn more about the scum he dealt with. No one with a brain would take the ramblings of a senile old woman over the word of a decorated police officer.''

He paused. "But…she got panicky and things got out of hand, and I…I guess I shoved her. I didn't mean to.''

But he had, and now Anna Mae was dead.

Chad moved closer, his face lined with remorse. "Now you know. I'm glad in a way. I've wanted to tell you for a long time. It's wrong to keep secrets from the people you love.''

Chills ran down Kristin's spine as she realized he wasn't sane. How had he kept it a secret for so long? She spoke quietly. "Chad, we should be going now.''

"Where?''

"Back to town. It's getting late, and I…I'm expecting a call from Rachel.''

He pursed his lips thoughtfully, then shook his head. "No, I think we should stay right here. I still owe you an apology.''

"For what?'' she asked, though she knew.

"For running into you on the attic stairs. For torching your shop. That gave me no pleasure, Kristin. And it wouldn't have been necessary if you had let me toss the journals in the trash that night.'' He released another lung-clearing sigh. "And my last apology is for what I have to do now.''

Chad shifted his stance, blocking the path to the open doorway, and Kristin's heart catapulted into her throat. "Did you happen to notice the rowboats down by the long dock? They're not even tied, just pulled up on shore. If we took one out on the water to enjoy the moonlight, no one would even care.''

He won't hurt me, she told herself. *He cares about me.* But they were empty words.

"I do love you," he said calmly. "But not enough to give up my freedom. I'm not going to jail, Kristin. I'm afraid there's going to be an accident.''

Lightning fast, Kristin scooped the chest from the floor, hurled it at his face and bolted for the doorway. She heard it crash to the concrete as Chad swore and ran after her. He caught her by the arm—yanked her back to him. Whirling to face him, Kristin brought her spike heel down hard on his instep, then rebounded with a knee to his groin. Roaring obscenities, Chad dropped like a stone, clawing at her on the way down.

She kicked off her heels and raced for the car. He'd left the keys in the ignition! She'd seen them! She could get away!

Whimpering, she grabbed the door handle and yanked it open, but he was coming again.

Chad lunged for her, knocking her to the dirt and gravel. He pinned her body beneath him and she screamed again.

"Shut up!" he yelled, but she kept screaming. "Shut the hell up! You're just making it worse!"

Kristin's mind went white-hot with rage. Was she supposed to just let him kill her? "No!" she cried. "No!" With all her strength, Kristin yanked her right hand free and slashed his face with her fingernails.

The last sound she heard before her world went black was his cry of rage as he rammed his fist into the side of her head.

Chapter 16

Zach swerved into the lot in a spray of gravel and skidded to stop near Chad's Blazer. He rushed from the truck and into the lighted bay.

His heart stopped when he saw everything tossed around helter-skelter. Something *was* wrong. She wouldn't have left it like this. Then he saw the photographs on the floor, recognized Chad, and swearing, bolted for the parking lot again.

He looked right and left, his senses sharpened to needle points as he listened for a sound—any sound that would give him direction. They couldn't have gone far. Chad's car was still here. Then he heard something in the night's stillness. *The splash of oars.*

Zach ran for the water like a man possessed—hit a muddy spot and skidded down the slight hill. He regained his balance and kept running. Moonlight on the lake was dim, but light poles glowed some distance away, closer to the marina. As he reached the long, clattering metal dock at a flat-out run, he spotted a lone rower fifty or sixty yards out and his heart pounded fiercely. He didn't need intuition to know the man was Chad, and that Kristin was in the boat. He made a split-second decision.

Praying she was all right, calling on every ounce of strength, Zach sped to the end of the dock and dove into the cold, spring-fed water. He came up stroking and thanking God he was a strong swimmer—thanking God the length of the dock cut the distance between him and Hollister in half.

The water pulled at his clothes, and he kept swimming, knowing he was vulnerable, but knowing that Chad would be no match for him if he could get him in the water. Hollister was cursing now, shouting something Zach couldn't make out. He was only a few yards from the boat when Chad scrambled to his feet and raised an oar.

"You just can't keep your nose out of my business, can you?" he screamed.

"Damn you, if you've hurt her—" Zach yelled hoarsely.

The oar came at him—chopped the water mere inches from his head. He dove under the boat, swam to the front and surfaced to fill his lungs, then dipped beneath the water again. Adrenaline screamed through his bloodstream. He felt the boat's underside, gauged Chad's rapid movements as Hollister moved about searching for him. When Chad moved, Zach moved, dipping beneath the water, then surfacing again in another spot.

Then Hollister's weight shifted to the port side.

Zach exploded to the surface and grabbed the side

of the boat—rocked it hard—and Hollister fell, shrieking, into the water.

But he recovered quickly and went for Zach's throat. Zach kicked him away, then dove and came up behind him, catching him in a vice grip around the neck.

Powerless, Chad clawed at Zach's hair and eyes, and Zach tightened his hold. But struggling as they were, it was impossible to stay afloat. Chad pulled them down into the blackness.

A new terror gripped Zach as Chad continued to flail and kick at him, keeping him from resurfacing. Hollister wasn't giving up. In that moment, Zach knew he'd drown them both before he let himself be taken.

Zach's feet hit the bottom. It was only eight or nine feet deep! Chad dug his fingers between his neck and Zach's arm, trying to break his hold, grunting his rage as air bubbles gurgled to the top.

Then, without warning, he went limp.

Grabbing the front of Chad's shirt, Zach pushed hard off the bottom and propelled them both to the surface, gulping in lifesaving air. Chad coughed and spit, only half-conscious.

Dragging him along, Zach side-stroked for the boat, then heaved himself up to see over the side.

She lay in the bottom, silent and still.

Tears stung his eyes and his heart crumbled. Heaven help him, he couldn't tell if she was breathing or not.

Choked by fear, he bobbed with Chad to the front of the boat and grabbed the towline, then with an arm under Chad's chin, kicked hard for the shallows.

Minutes later, gasping, he dragged Chad, then the boat, onto the bank and staggered back to check on Kristin. He was nearly overcome by emotion when he realized she was still alive, then heartsick again when he couldn't rouse her.

Digging his pocket knife from his wet jeans, he cut the tow line and quickly tied Chad's hands and ankles together, then scrambled up the hill to his truck. It killed him to leave her, but he couldn't take a chance on moving her. He didn't know what her injuries were.

Only now beginning to shake, Zach snatched his cell phone from the seat to call an ambulance and the state police. Then he raced back to Kristin's side and prayed for all he was worth.

Paramedics were just pushing her gurney into the hospital's emergency room when Kristin's lashes fluttered, and she opened her eyes. Zach's irritation with the medics who hadn't let him ride with her vanished.

"Hi," he said, relief flooding through him. "How do you feel?"

She tried to talk, then moistened her lips and tried again. "My head hurts. What…what am I doing here? Is this…a hospital?"

"All things in good time," Zach murmured. "We'll talk after the doctor checks you out." He bent to kiss her softly. "I'll be in the waiting room. I'll see you as soon as I can."

The ambulance driver motioned to Zach's shirt and jeans. "You'll have time to change to dry clothes if you want. They'll probably order X-rays, and the cops are on their way to take her statement."

Zach shook his head. "I'm not going anywhere."

Forty minutes later, he dragged a chair close to her bed in a curtained-off cubicle in the emergency room. She had a concussion and was still dealing with a headache, but the CAT scan showed no bleeding or fractures, and she remembered everything that had happened.

"They're keeping me overnight for observation," she said after she'd repeated the story she'd told the state police. "My doctor's an alarmist."

"I'm glad," Zach replied and squeezed her hand. "You were unconscious for a long time."

Remembered fear flickered through her eyes. "He would've killed me," she said quietly. "You saved my life."

Zach smiled and kissed her hand. "I had to. I love you."

The grave look she sent him before she turned away said she didn't believe it.

"Don't do that," he said gently, turning her face back to him. "I do love you. I always have. Kris, I want you to be my wife."

"What happened to your plans to own the world?"

"If you marry me, I'll have it."

Tears welled in her eyes, and she shook her head.

"Why? Is it still about Gretchen?"

"No. I've put that behind me. We were young...and you might have been right about my finding excuses not to marry you. I just don't know for sure."

"Then why?"

"Zach, you're not ready for a station wagon and a white picket fence. You've told me that a dozen times in a dozen different ways. Even your old girlfriends know that."

"What old girlfriends?" he asked, then with a trace of impatience, said, "What did Stephanie tell you?"

"Nothing that I didn't already know. You're a workaholic. You're driven. I saw the change that came over you when I was at your beach house. I can't compete with that. More to the point, I don't want to."

"Kris—"

"I want a man who's content to put in a normal day's work and spend the rest of his time with his family. You work from dusk till dark. I want children, and kids need a father who's willing to give them time when they're young—not hand them a brimming bank account and a thriving business after they've missed trips to ball games and picnics on Sunday afternoons."

"I can change," he said, working to keep the desperation out of his voice. "I never had a reason to come home before."

But one look at her told him she didn't believe that, either. "Do you love me?"

"Yes. Even when it hurt to think of you, I loved you. I just don't—"

She stopped, but Zach knew how to finish the sentence. "You just don't trust me. Not to keep my word, and not to change my priorities."

"You are what you are. I know how badly you need to prove to yourself that you're nothing like your father. If working yourself sick is the only way you can do it...I think you'll do it."

He couldn't reply for a long time. The lump in his throat wouldn't let him. How ironic that he'd finally realized what he wanted, what he needed, and she wasn't having any part of it.

Standing, he squeezed her hand again, then backed away. "Get some rest," he said softly. "I'll come by in the morning to take you home."

But she was shaking her head again. "Thank you, but I think it would be better if I made my own arrangements."

"That's it, then?" he asked, unwilling to believe it. "We're over?"

When she didn't answer after several moments, Zach nodded grimly and took a few more backward steps. Then there was nothing to do but leave.

The days ahead were crushing. Finding the energy to go through the motions of living was a major accomplishment. But the insurance check came, and Kristin forced herself to plan her future. She arranged to have the lot cleared, poured over catalogs and ads in search of new pieces, and phoned Jeremy Sherwood to accept the first floor plan he'd shown her. She did everything she could to put Zach out of her mind. Still, he was there in her dreams—smiling and holding her and kissing her as though he had a right to.

A full week later, her phone rang as she was carrying her cereal bowl to the sink. When Etta Gardner asked how she was, Kristin had to lie. "I'm fine, Mrs. Gardner. You?"

"Well, actually, I'm more than a little concerned," Etta said in a troubled voice.

Kristin's first thought was that Zach had been hurt. Her heart fell to the floor. "Why? Has something happened?"

"Not exactly. But Zachary just called to tell me he'd left a very expensive surprise at the farmhouse, and I can't pick it up because my car's in the shop. I wouldn't ask you, but Bertie doesn't drive, and Annabelle just lost her license." Etta hesitated, then continued in a downcast voice, "But if you have other things to do right now and can't spare the time, I'll understand."

Kristin stifled a sigh. She couldn't lie to her. "No,

I'm not busy right now. I'd be glad to get it for you. How will I know what it is?''

"Well, he said it's gift-wrapped and sitting on the kitchen counter. The house is locked, but there's a key taped behind the light on the back porch.''

"Zach's gone?'' Kristin asked tentatively.

"He finished with the house three days ago,'' Etta said kindly. "Was there something you wanted to say to him?''

There were a thousand things she'd wanted to say to him, but none of them made any sense. She'd made the best decision she could, for both of them. "No. No, nothing,'' she replied, swallowing. "I'll see you in a half hour or so.''

She knew it would be difficult, going to the farmhouse, but she had no idea just how difficult. Memories rushed at her from every corner as Kristin parked her van in the empty driveway and walked around back to the porch. The smell of cut lumber, the freshly painted railings and posts—even the patches of sawdust in the grass were all reminders that she didn't need. The old memories were just as disturbing, and pretty promises whispered to her from the trees near the pond, from the loft in the big barn. *You're every dream I've ever had, Kris. Every wish I've ever made.*

Silencing them with a shake of her head, she climbed the steps. The key was taped to the outside light as Etta had promised. Kristin removed it, inserted it into the lock, then bracing herself, opened the door. She'd be okay. She just had to get this over with and go back home.

Tears sprang to her eyes the instant she saw the

ribbon draped package sitting on the countertop. All six-feet-two-inches of him.

She walked right back out.

Zach came after her, turning her around before she could leave the porch, and meeting her eyes with equal parts candor and sincerity. "I'm selling my business to Dan, and moving back here to start a new one. I love you and I want to marry you."

Kristin shook her head. "Zach—"

"Hear me out before you start spouting excuses why it won't work. Please?"

He was so passionate, she had to give him that courtesy.

Soberly, he handed her a package she hadn't realized he was holding. It was one that she'd gift-wrapped herself, except the paper had been loosened and retaped. "It's the music box," she said.

"Open it."

Wary, Kristin met his gaze, then glanced down to remove the paper and hold the pretty filigreed box in her hands. The feelings that moved through her were bittersweet. Untouched by the fire, it shone silver and perfect in the morning light. Like her, it had only survived because Zach had kept it safe.

The tinkling melody began to play as he lifted the lid and withdrew a thin coil of nylon rope from inside the box, then gave it to her. Kristin looked at it, not quite understanding, then met his eyes again.

"If you'll marry me," he said quietly, "I swear that you and our kids will always be my first priority. Every day, in every way. But if I ever forget that— and I know I won't—you can use this to roust me from any meeting or construction site, any time of the day or night, and lead me back where I belong. With you."

Tears slid over her cheeks as Kristin studied the resolve and conviction in his eyes. Could he give it all up? His home, the company he'd built, his friends? Her heart took a hopeful little skip. "Zach, you have to be sure. I couldn't handle it if you did another about-face."

"I've never been more sure of anything. I need you and I want you, and we've wasted so much time—"

Kristin hurled herself into his waiting arms, an overwhelming joy filling her. "Yes! Oh, yes, I'll marry you. And you don't have to sell your business. I can live anywhere as long as I'm with you."

"No, you love it here," he murmured, rocking her close. "And Etta's waited a long time for this. She'd string me up if we had kids and she couldn't see them when she wanted to."

"But you said Nags Head was home."

Zach eased her away and cupped her face in his hands, smiling as he smoothed her tears away. "Nags Head is where I live," he said tenderly. "Home is where you are."

Kristin's tears began to roll again, and Zach smiled. Then he kissed her deeply, and it was a kiss filled with promise and a heartfelt pledge for their future. But more than that, Kristin thought as she melted in his arms, the kiss was every dream she'd ever had. Every wish she'd ever made.

Epilogue

A warm ocean breeze blew through the bedroom's screened patio door as Kristin and Zach lay spooned together in the rumpled sheets. Their left hands were linked, and matching gold wedding bands caught the first early rays of Carolina sunlight. Outside, only the crash of frothy breakers interrupted the morning silence.

Eyes closed, Kristin smiled as Zach's voice rustled, thick with sleep, beside her ear. "Have I told you that I love you yet this morning?"

"I think you said something like that around 4:00 a.m.," she replied groggily, snuggling his arms more tightly around her. "But I was busy and I'm not sure I heard right. Maybe you should tell me again."

"Nah, I don't want to spoil you. First thing you know, you'll expect me to say it every day for the next hundred years."

Laughing, she flounced around and shoved him onto

his back. "Say it, or you're not leaving this bed today."

"That's some threat," he returned, chuckling. Then he gathered her close and kissed her forehead. "I love you from the tips of your hair to the bottoms of your feet. And I *will* tell you that every day for the next hundred years." He stroked her arm, then craned his neck to kiss her lightly on the lips. "Know what feels good?"

Laughing, Kristin said, "Yes."

He laughed, too. "Well, it does, but I was thinking what a relief it is that all the turmoil and craziness is behind us. It feels so good to lie here and know that the peace I'm feeling isn't going to end in ten minutes, and we'll have to try again to find our way back to each other."

"You bet," she agreed through a sigh.

Everything had been resolved in some way. Chad was in jail and awaiting trial…Etta had been utterly delighted to give Zach away at their wedding last week…and Rachel had taken one look at Kristin's beaming face, cast aside her doubts and welcomed Zach into their tiny family. When she and Dan Perkins stood for them as maid of honor and best man, Rachel was one hundred percent behind the marriage.

"Ready to go back home tomorrow?" Kristin asked, a little sad that their time here was over. Although, Zach's lease was only up in January, so they could certainly come back a few times before then.

"Yes and no. I like this honeymoon stuff, but we need to get a crew together and start your shop if you want to be open by Thanksgiving. That only gives us four months."

He'd said *we*, she thought, smiling. *We* need to get a crew together. "Our first collaboration."

Chuckling again, Zach brought his hand down to span her flat stomach. "Don't you mean, second?"

She nodded, then turned to meet his eyes, so grateful for everything they'd been through because all the hard times had made each new happiness even sweeter. While no one was paying attention, a new little life had begun. A new little life who would have both a doting mommy and a hands-on daddy.

"Did I ever tell you about the daydream I had about you and a little girl running along the beach?" he asked.

"No, but it sounds nice." Everything except the word 'beach' because it dampened her joy a bit. "Zach, are you sure about this move? I keep thinking about the beautiful home you planned to build here."

Rolling to his side, he grinned down at her. "I can build that house just as easily in Pennsylvania."

"On stilts?"

"I don't need stilts to make me happy. All I want and need is what I already have. You and the baby."

"Good," she whispered, slipping her arms around his neck. "Because all we need is you. Now give me a real kiss."

They'd been given a precious gift, a second chance at love few people were lucky enough to glimpse even a first time. To endure, it needed to be nurtured and treasured, guarded and cherished. But as their lips sealed and contented sighs broke the stillness of their bedroom, Kristin knew they were up to the task.

* * * * *

CODE NAME: **DANGER**

The action continues with the men—and women—of the Omega Agency in Merline Lovelace's *Code Name: Danger* series.

This August, in TEXAS HERO (IM #1165) a renegade is assigned to guard his former love, a historian whose controversial theories are making her sorely in need of protection. But who's going to protect *him*—from her? A couple struggles with their past as they hope for a future....

And coming soon, more *Code Name: Danger* stories from Merline Lovelace....

Code Name: Danger
Because love is a risky business...

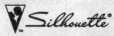

COMING NEXT MONTH